"It's me you want, Paula," Hugo said

"When you told me last night that you loved me, you meant it. It had nothing to do with shock, deny it all you like."

"I do deny it," Paula shot back, not meeting his eyes. "I was drunk."

"Not so drunk you didn't enjoy everything I did to you," Hugo said coolly. "And you weren't drunk the night I came back, when you wanted me to make love to you." He looked down at her, his smile taunting.

"Then you should have taken the opportunity while you had it," she shouted, her face on fire.

Hugo laughed. "Oh, no. When we make love, it's going to be because we both want to, Paula, not because your frustrations get the better of you and you can't help yourself."

Edwina Shore spent thirteen years working in Australia's publishing community, editing mainly academic work, with a few brief forays into general trade or "best-seller" publishing. Now, when she isn't immersed in her own writing, she tries to work in her other interests, which include travel to Great Britain, Europe and throughout Australia, learning Scottish Gaelic, sculpting and painting. She is single and lives in Victoria.

Books by Edwina Shore

HARLEQUIN ROMANCE
2753—A WILL TO LOVE

The Last Barrier

Edwina Shore

Harlequin Books

TORONTO • NEW YORK • LONDON
AMSTERDAM • PARIS • SYDNEY • HAMBURG
STOCKHOLM • ATHENS • TOKYO • MILAN

Original hardcover edition published in 1986
by Mills & Boon Limited

ISBN 0-373-02798-2

Harlequin Romance first edition November 1986

CHAPTER ONE

PAULA sat on the bench against the rough stone wall of the cottage. The blank page of the sketch-pad on her lap gleamed white in the late afternoon sunlight—but unthreateningly. And that was the difference five weeks on the island had made: a blank page was just a blank page and not the end of the world. Tomorrow she might fill it; then again, she might not. Lazily contented, Paula leaned back and watched the child.

Jamie lay on the ground a few feet away, engrossed in stacking stones of varying sizes into some mysterious shape that presumably had its counterpart in his imagination. He was a small dark wisp of a boy; a Celtic child with his pale skin and dark blue eyes under the crop of black curls. Paula found she could look at him without any image of Stephen rearing in her mind and that was something she wouldn't have believed possible when she first arrived on the island and discovered him staying with his grandfather at the main house.

Then, every small boy, any shape or size, was still a painful reminder of Stephen, and Paula had been furious that her publisher hadn't told her about Jamie when he organised her stay on the island. If she had known about the child she wouldn't have come, and that was probably why

5

Roger hadn't told her. Mild subterfuge perhaps, but for someone so invariably predictable during all the years Paula had known him, Roger had suddenly taken to acting startlingly out of character.

He had astounded her at their lunch six weeks ago when she handed over her illustrations for the new children's book his company was about to publish. Her first attempt since the car crash, Paula's heart and soul had gone into them and she had sat back, expecting ... what? Approval ...? Delighted congratulations ...? Roger's reaction shocked her speechless.

The kind, concerned friend who had gently bullied her into taking the commission in the first place turned into a stranger who lashed her ruthlessly about reproducing stuff she had done years ago, about using Stephen as the model for the small body in the book.

'Stephen's dead,' Roger had stated cruelly, 'and sticking him into every book from now to Kingdom Come won't bring him back to life. He's wrong for this book, Paula, and if you can't see that, you'd better think about another line of work, because the Paula Halstead who was on her way to becoming one of the top illustrators in the business doesn't exist anymore.'

Paula hadn't been able to believe her ears. 'It's a year since the accident Paula—time enough to pull yourself together and get over things,' Roger told her with that same calculated cruelty, and Paula had never hated anyone as she did Roger Harris at that moment. What did Roger know about 'getting over things'? She had caused the accident which had taken the life of her fiancé and his four-year-old son, and that wasn't something a year—or any number of years—could wipe out. Mark's death she might have coped with, but a child's . . .? Was it any wonder it was Stephen's little face she had drawn on every page willy-nilly?

'You need to get away for a while and I know just the place,' Roger said, and Paula had heard that before—a lot. Ever since she had recovered from the accident—physically at any rate—everyone was always trying to pack her off somewhere. Glazed-eyed, Paula had listened to countless versions of 'just the place'; Italy was her mother's panacea for anything from a cold to a nervous breakdown, but there had been Spanish beaches, Swiss mountains, she had rejected them all.

And Roger's version?

A remote Scottish island. Peace, quiet, no distractions; no memories of Mark and Stephen was what he meant of course. And the way Roger put it, she would practically be doing his old friend Sir Iain Cameron a favour by staying in the cottage on Sir Iain's estate for a couple of months. The retired heart specialist had recently lost a son and daughter-in-law in an air disaster in America and would be grateful for her company.

The selling points were mere formality. Having just shocked the daylights out of her, Roger could have packed her off anywhere he chose, and it was just as well his friend only lived off the coast of Scotland and not Africa, Paula thought with a wry smile as she put the sketch-pad on the bench and felt her hair. It was almost dry. She ran her fingers through the curls to ruffle the last moisture out of them and thought idly about getting her hair cut, but it seemed too much trouble.

Mark had liked her hair very short—a curly red-gold cap close to her head. He said the style brought out the gold flecks in her green eyes, but the artist in her saw it was wrong and disliked it. At five feet eight, she was too tall for such a small cap of hair but had given in and worn it that way to please him. There had been other things she had given in about. A shutter clicked down in her mind. She did not want to think about Mark. Paula sighed audibly and Jamie lifted his head.

'Will Uncle Hugo come today?' he asked—as he asked almost every day and probably not just of her; his grandfather, Anna the housekeeper and even Neil, the odd-job man, must have come in for their share of the heartbreaking question.

Paula smiled down at the upturned face and gave a small shrug. 'You'll have to ask your grandfather.' Her standard answer.

'I did ask him,' Jamie muttered stonily. 'He said Uncle Hugo didn't tell him.'

'Then it will be a lovely surprise when he does come, won't it?' Paula said lightly, resenting the uncle who could so casually leave a small boy waiting without a word.

Jamie gave her a long searching look. The penetrating gaze of the dark velvety eyes made Paula uncomfortable. Her comment had been patronising and the boy deserved better than that—if only the truth.

'I'm sorry Jamie, I just don't know when your uncle will come. But I'm sure it must be very soon now,' she added in spite of herself because she couldn't bear the blank, distancing look that came into the child's eyes.

Jamie dropped his eyes from her face. A deliberate sweep of the small hand scattered the carefully-balanced construction into an untidy heap of stones. He got to his feet and without a word started down the path to the water.

Paula watched him go with despairing help-lessness. There was no point in calling him back because she couldn't give the answer he wanted any more than his grandfather; only Hugo Cameron could do that and he apparently chose not to.

She had held back from questioning Sir Iain about his son's absence, but concern for Jamie, and, Paula had to admit, an element of curiosity, had made her broach the subject with the housekeeper.

'It's not that he doesn't want the lad,' Anna hastily assured her. 'Jamie is his own brother's son after all, but its barely three months since the tragedy and there is still so much Mr Hugo has to attend to, putting things into trust for Jamie and the good Lord only knows what else. It's a mercy Mr Hugo is such a fine businessman, else it would take forever, what with all the extra work his brother's death has created for him. Mind you, he did have the boy with him in London for the first month but it wasn't easy for a man in his position so he thought it would be best for everybody if the lad stayed with Sir Iain awhile.

When Mr Hugo gets back from America he'll be making more permanent arrangements.'

To suit his own convenience and never mind about Jamie. Paula managed to restrain herself from voicing her conclusions aloud, but the picture built up in her mind; she thought Hugo Cameron a monstrously selfish man and took Anna's indulgent explanations with a very large pinch of salt. To hear the old housekeeper talk, 'Mr Hugo' ran financial empires single-handed and in his spare time walked on water.

Paula got up abruptly and wandered down the path. Jamie had not gone far and she saw him immediately she rounded the small slope that blocked the view of the sea from her cottage. He was sitting on a rock a short way up the beach, waiting for her. His face brightened as she reached him. 'Are you coming to the house for dinner this evening?' he asked, by way of telling her that his little fit of depression was over.

'Yes, your grandfather has asked me,' Paula replied with a smile.

'Oh good. I shall come and call for you. I like coming to call for you,' he added shyly.

'I like it too.'

Escorting her to the house on the evenings she dined there made him feel grown-up and important, but it made Paula sad and at the same time unaccountably angry that such a small thing should be such a highlight in his life. She turned away so he wouldn't see the expression on her face. 'Come on, Jamie, let's play follow-my-leader.'

They took it in turns to lead the way, jumping

from rock to rock in the green shallows, the leader selecting the most difficult rocks. The one who slipped off into the water the least times won, and it was a moot point as to which of them derived the more enjoyment from the simple game. 'Larking about' Mark would have called it—and disapproved.

Paula jumped off the last rock of the outcrop and Jamie followed, laughing at her heels. 'We'll call it a draw. Home now, Jamie, it's getting too chilly to stay any longer and Anna will have to clean you up before dinner. Your jeans are soaked.'

'So are yours,' he retorted cheekily. 'Race you back to the house.' He grinned—more gaps than teeth, and started sprinting lightly across the sand in the direction of the path to the main house. Paula gave him a head start then set off after him.

At the top of the slope where the ground levelled out and the solid two-storey stone house came into view, there was a rough stretch of path before it became smoother again closer to the house. Jamie was intent on picking his way over the uneven stony surface which was why Paula saw the car before he did, and stopped in her tracks.

She had never seen anything like it. Forced to guess, she would have said it was one of those fantastic Italian jobs, but low and sleek, all curves and glass, the navy sports-car looked as exotically alien as a spaceship. Who in their right mind would bring a car like that on to an island which boasted a main street about the width of a London alley? 'Uncle Hugo is here!' Paula heard

Jamie suddenly shriek. 'Uncle Hugo', who else? And if that was Uncle Hugo's style then she disliked it as much as she already disliked the man.

Jamie stood transfixed until she reached him. 'Uncle Hugo is here,' he repeated, and seemed so stunned he could barely get the strangled whisper out. He grabbed her hand. 'Hurry Paula, Uncle Hugo is here,' he squeaked again and together they ran past the car to the house.

The front door was ajar. Jamie flung himself against it like a miniature whirlwind. 'Easy, Jamie,' Paula laughed, trying to catch her breath as he literally dragged her into the spacious hall, a room in itself with the large open fireplace facing the front door.

The man crossing the hall turned at the commotion they made, then stopped and they all just stood there and stared at each other.

Her vicious mental picture of 'Uncle Hugo' had not included any physical details, but Paula would have recognised the man in front of her a mile off. It was like seeing the Sir Iain of thirty years ago—or Jamie thirty years on, a tall powerfully-built man, with the bones of his face more pronounced, the nose and jaw stronger but with that same remarkable colouring. Only surely without that hardness in the handsome face?

It was a long, awkward moment; Hugo Cameron at one end of the hall, she and Jamie at the other, the child gripping her hand with excruciating fierceness. Hugo Cameron made the first move—a sudden gesture, abruptly raising his hands as if he was opening his arms to the child. He dropped them again as Jamie stayed rooted to the spot. The boy might have been fretting for his uncle, but face to face with him at last was acting as if he was terrified of the man.

'Do you plan on staying there all day?' There was an edge to the smooth voice that carried no trace of his father's brogue.

Paula unprised the vice-like little fingers and gave Jamie a gentle push. Set into motion, he strode towards the man, almost bravely, and held out his hand. 'Hello, Uncle Hugo,' he said formally, in a low unsteady voice, with his head lowered and eyes fixed somewhere around his uncle's feet.

Paula winced. Any other child would have hurled himself at the man like an excited puppy. Not Jamie. Hugo Cameron's nephew feared rejection too much and had waited too long to risk it.

They shook hands with a solemnity that might have amused her if it hadn't been so heart-rendingly pathetic. Jamie finally took his eyes off his uncle's shoes and Hugo suddenly smiled down at him. From across the hall the eyes looked as black as the eyebrows and the wayward lock of hair above them, but closer, Paula knew they would be the same startling dark blue as the child's. As Hugo smiled they lit up, relaxing the hardness of his face and giving it an unexpected warmth. He put his hand to the boy's head and ran his fingers through the springy black curls that resembled his own. 'Hello, young man,' he said gently.

She hadn't realised she had been holding her breath. Paula felt herself relax. There was affection in the man's gesture and in his voice.

She felt vaguely reassured and could only hope that Jamie felt the same way.

Hugo raised his eyes to her over Jamie's head. The warmth which had lit up their dark depths when he smiled at the child was so very definitely absent Paula wondered if she had imagined it. They ranged over her unhurriedly, with casual but unmistakable expertise. It was a blatantly sexual appraisal and Hugo Cameron made no attempt to disguise that from her.

As his eyes returned to her face, Paula stiffened with hostility, heat streaking her cheeks as she tried to push back the rising consciousness of her untidy mass of wind-blown curls, the shapeless sweater and damp jeans above the inelegant Wellingtons. She stared back stonily, irritatingly aware she presented a picture of overgrown ragamuffin while in his superbly cut navy slacks and camel-toned pullover, Hugo Cameron could have stepped out of the pages of a fashion magazine—too smooth and suave by half; Paula wished he'd step right back into them and disappear from sight.

Jamie moved to his uncle's side and gave her a blissful beam. 'This is my Uncle Hugo.' He effected his childish introduction with the air of an amateur magician pulling a rabbit out of a hat—with desperate panache and a grateful relief that it had been in there at all.

Hugo's mouth gave a quirk at the boy's proud announcement. 'And who's your friend, Jamie?' he queried drily.

Paula was livid at being addressed through the child.

'Paula. She's pretty, isn't she?' Jamie looked up

anxiously at his uncle for confirmation of his statement.

'Yes. Very pretty.' The cool voice agreed smoothly while the eyes took in her growing discomfort with something that looked very much like satisfaction.

Paula hated being called pretty. She was not pretty; unusual-looking, yes. The upward slant of the almond-shaped eyes were paralleled by the long line of the eyebrows; the nose was straight but her mouth she had always considered too wide and the bottom lip too full. Her colouring was the most striking feature and the bones were in the right place, as her sculptor mother would say. The overall effect was interesting but it needed more than a casual glance, no matter how expert, to pick that up. The child's assessment was innocent enough; the man's comment strictly patronising and meant to embarrass.

Paula unfroze her face into marginally less antagonistic lines for Jamie's sake. 'I'm sure Jamie is very happy to see you—at last, Mr Cameron.' She squeezed the words out through her teeth and turned with a sweep to the door.

'Just a moment ... Paula.' Her name was included as an afterthought and with a deliberate familiarity that made her bristle.

Paula reversed her turn. 'Yes, Mr Cameron?' she bit out frostily and was pleased to note from the momentary scowl that she'd hit the right tone of voice—the one that needled him.

Hugo's mouth tightened into a thin straight line of displeasure. 'The boy needs a bath,' he said with clipped coldness.

Completely taken aback, all Paula could do was agree. 'Yes, he does.' Jamie usually needed a bath and a change of clothes after one of their more exuberant sessions on the beach and Anna usually gave him one.

'Then I suggest you take him upstairs and give him one,' Hugo snapped, pushing Jamie towards her. Paula was too astonished to react. 'You look as if you could do with one yourself,' Hugo observed drily, his mouth giving a satisfied twist as the impertinence hit home. Flaring like a beacon, Paula opened her mouth and shut it again.

'See to the child.' Hugo gave a curt nod of dismissal and walked away leaving Paula speechless.

On the point of a seizure, she watched him disappear through the doorway into the living-room and then it was all she could do to stop herself lunging after him, and demanding to know just who the hell he thought he was to be speaking to her like that—or more to the point, who did he think she was?

The answer was fairly obvious when the consuming fury died down to a low seething burn: he had taken her for a maid, or Jamie's nanny. Well, there were worse things to be taken for and that wasn't what made Paula so furious— it was the sheer arrogance and familiarity accompanying the assumption that took her breath away.

Jamie looked up, eyes clouded with puzzlement and hurt, the scene he had just witnessed way beyond his comprehension. Paula put a not-very-steady hand on his rigid little shoulder. 'Perhaps we had better do what your uncle wants, Jamie,' she said in a voice so controlled she amazed herself.

It was a quick bath and quick change into clean clothes—all achieved without a word. Jamie might not have understood what had gone on downstairs—Paula wasn't sure she understood herself—but the child was hurt and she could sense that part of his silent reproach was directed at her, as if she too had somehow failed him.

And in a way he was right. She had unwittingly created the unhappy situation just by being there. Hugo Cameron had been much too sharp to miss her antagonism and had gone out of his way to needle her and while she hadn't done much more than glare her dislike, the result was the same as if they had engaged in an all-out slanging match. And poor Jamie had suffered for it.

Paula ran a comb through his damp hair. 'There now, you'd better go and show yourself to your uncle again.'

Jamie gave her an expressionless stare. 'I hate him,' he said, very quietly and without any emotion.

Paula said nothing. She understood how he felt and when downstairs outside the door to the living-room he clung to her hand and pleaded 'Please come in with me, Paula,' she couldn't find it in herself to refuse.

Head thrown back, eyes closed, Hugo was stretched out in an armchair by the fireplace where the peat burnt warmly; mid-May brought no guarantee of warmth to the island, and Anna laid the fire daily. The long, powerful frame swamped Sir Iain's favourite chair but his son seemed totally at ease in it and surprisingly, very much part of the warm, mellow room. Paula felt an unreasonable stirring of resentment to see him blend in so easily—as if he belonged. She thought he was asleep until Hugo flicked his eyes open, and moving his head slightly met her eyes.

'Your nephew has been given a bath—as ordered,' she said tightly, and tried out a waxy smile on him. If he thought she was Jamie's nanny, she would act the part for him.

'A decided improvement,' Hugo smiled—at the child, then swept a quick look over her. Paula glared him a dare to comment on her own unaltered appearance but he passed up the challenge and turned his head towards the far end of the room—to the woman standing in the deeply-recessed bay of the large front window. Paula wondered how she could have possibly missed noticing her.

'This is my nephew, Louise . . . James's son.' Hugo motioned Jamie towards the woman. 'Go and say how-do-you-do to Miss Hunt, Jamie.'

Jamie dutifully crossed the room to the elegant brunette in the russet suede slacks with a matching jacket draped loosely over a white silk shirt.

'It's lovely to meet you, Jamie,' she murmured in a low husky voice, and ignoring Jamie's extended hand, reached out to ruffle his hair

Dropping his hand, Jamie stepped back abruptly—quite rudely, out of her reach, and Miss Hunt's smile was momentarily superceded by a flash of dislike. Then shrugging elegantly, she dropped her own hand and turned her eyes on Paula—or rather, Paula surmised, returned them; the woman must have been watching her all the time.

Paula met the bland stare with a slight smile and might have saved her muscles the bother; it went completely unacknowledged. The beautifully made-up eyes looked right through her before Louise Hunt lifted her ever-so-slightly too-prominent chin and looked away. The airy little snub left Paula white with outrage. She did not have to stand for this sort of treatment from anybody. 'If you'll excuse me,' she said with a civility that almost choked her and turned to the door.

'Wait!' Hugo Cameron shot the word at her back. Paula froze. The urge to ignore him and flounce out of the room was overpowering and for a split second she thought she would. But she turned around slowly, deliberately keeping her hand on the door knob. She didn't speak because she wasn't sure she could be accountable for any words that came out of her mouth. Arching a shapely eyebrow with all the haughtiness she could produce, Paula gave what Roger always called her fish-eyed stare. It was usually effective—it riled people no end, and Hugo Cameron was no exception. His eyes narrowed dangerously.

After the pause that went on for too long, he said icily, 'I'll want a word with you later—I'll let you know when it's convenient.'

Don't hold your breath, Paula would have

loved to have spat at him but didn't quite have
the nerve, and there was something about him
that made her feel quite glad she was not Jamie's
nanny after all. She made a non-committal
movement of her head that was open to any
interpretation he chose to put on it, then with a
glance and a quick smile at the miserable-looking
Jamie trapped by the window near Miss Hunt,
Paula walked out.

With remarkable restraint she closed the door
very quietly behind her—only because she sensed
the unbelievably arrogant man in the living-room
was expecting her to slam it and she was not
going to give him even that small satisfaction if
she could help it.

Just around the corner of the corridor off the
hall, Anna was saying something in in-
comprehensible but very loud Gaelic. To Paula's
consternation, Sir Iain's voice murmured a reply
a step closer. Another moment and they'd be
upon her and Sir Iain would insist on taking her
back into the living-room to introduce her
formally to his son. No thank you. She'd had
about as much of his disagreeable son as she
could stand for one day. Paula shot to the front
door.

A couple of hurried steps down the path she
stopped, suddenly remembering she was expected
to dine at the house that evening. Sit at table with
Hugo Cameron? She'd rather starve to death.
Paula hesitated. Make her excuses to Sir Iain now
or wait until later when she had calmed down a
little?

As she dithered, the front door opened and

slammed shut again. Paula spun around to see
Jamie flying down the steps towards her, his face
telling all. No longer his uncle's 'young man' he
was simply a very unhappy and hurt small boy,
and unthinkingly, Paula dropped to her knees and
let him run into her arms.

She held him close until his emotional spasm
passed then released him. 'Would you like me to
take you back inside now?'

Jamie gave an agitated shake of his head. 'No.
Uncle Hugo doesn't like me.'

It would have been easy to dismiss his
accusation with the pat adult 'nonsense'. She had
only his uncle's smile to go by, and the way he
had run his fingers through Jamie's hair, but
Paula sensed that despite his brusqueness Hugo
did like the boy. 'I think he does like you, Jamie.
You'll just have to give him more time to get used
to you again,' she said honestly. 'I'd like you to
go back now. Go and have a talk with your
grandfather, tell him how you feel.'

Jamie considered that carefully, then to Paula's
relief nodded. 'And will you please tell him that I
won't be able to come to dinner this evening,'
Paula added hurriedly.

He looked at her, moist eyes speaking volumes.
She was betraying him, deserting him. 'Another
evening Jamie, not tonight,' Paula said briskly.
'Please tell your grandfather that.' She bent down
suddenly and kissed him quickly on the cheek.
'Go on, now.'

Jamie's resolute obedience was painful to
watch. Paula followed him up the path with her
eyes and waited until he had closed the door

behind him before she turned—and found herself looking into Hugo Cameron's eyes through the living-room window. She started guiltily, a malicious heat flooding her cheeks, then jerked her eyes away and sped down the path, furious with herself for the idiotic reaction.

CHAPTER TWO

SHE was in the act of glancing at her watch when the tap on the door sounded. Eight o'clock on the dot. Jamie? Had he come for her after she had distinctly told him she wouldn't be dining at the house? Paula sighed in frustration; he probably hadn't even passed on her message to his grandfather.

She put down the book she had been attempting to read without much success. She could not concentrate and had Hugo Cameron to thank for that; he had made a very thorough job of ruffling her feathers and they refused to lie down. The most frustrating thing was that she kept thinking up all the snide, cutting retorts which had eluded her when she had been face to face with the rude man. Next time she'd be ready—if there had to be a next time.

Paula pattered to the door, determined to be very firm with the child. She was in slippers and her thick grey woollen dressing-gown after the bath that Hugo Cameron thought she had needed so badly, but not yet ready for bed. There were still hours to fill in before she could go to bed with any assurance of sleep; sleep was not something that came easily since the accident and Paula didn't want a night of tossing and turning which was the usual result if she went to bed too early.

'I hope I'm not disturbing you.' Sir Iain's tall, spare frame filled the doorway.

Paula swallowed her surprise and gave a quick shake of the head, wishing she had not flung the door open with such bad-tempered force. 'I wasn't expecting a visitor. Would you like to come in?' she invited uneasily, wondering what he was doing on her doorstep, and was relieved when Sir Iain shook his head. 'I hope Jamie gave you my message?' Paula asked, a little sharply.

'Yes, the lad did that,' Sir Iain assured her. 'And that's what I'd like to talk to you about.'

'I'd prefer not to come this evening, Sir Iain,' Paula anticipated quickly.

Sir Iain gave her a long look. 'I gather my son was rude to you this afternoon, Paula, and I've come to apologise on his behalf,' he said without preamble, and with a solemn sincerity that made Paula blush with embarrassment—mainly for the old gentleman standing in front of her. How dare Hugo use his father as an errand boy. 'That's very kind of you, Sir Iain,' she murmured, 'but really not necessary.'

'I think it is,' he corrected her gently. 'You're here as my guest and I won't have you upset. Hugo wanted to come himself.' He caught the flash of disbelief across her face and smiled faintly. 'I assure you he did, but I wouldn't let him, because, my dear, I felt he might not have succeeded in persuading you to join us for dinner.'

Very true, but she doubted his father would have any more success. 'I'd rather not,' Paula repeated firmly. 'Not this evening. It's a family occasion and you don't want me there, not on Mr Cameron's first evening and ...' She shrugged. And besides which, I can't stand your son, was what she actually had in mind.

'We do want you, or I wouldn't be asking.'

'We?' Paula repeated his plural, almost mockingly.

'Jamie, myself—and yes, Hugo.' Sir Iain's mouth gave a wry tilt—a softer version of his son's ready twist. 'I know he's not made a very good impression on you but he really would like the opportunity to make amends.'

And Paula could guess how—by laying on the charm with a trowel. Hugo Cameron would be very adept at that—men like him always were. It didn't require too much stretch of the imagination to visualise the dark blue eyes crinkling in a disarming smile—but not missing a trick; they'd be carefully gauging the effect on the victim at the same time. Well, the charming Mr Cameron would have to practise his art on someone else tonight. Miss Hunt?

'I'd rather not. Thank you for coming to apologise—on Mr Cameron's behalf.' Paula sounded more stiffly formal than she intended.

The old man frowned at her unexpected intransigence. 'It was an honest mistake, Paula. Hugo told me he mistook you for a local girl caring for Jamie, and I imagine he treated you accordingly.' He allowed himself a rueful smile. 'I'm afraid Hugo does have a tendency to order people about at the best of times and just recently he's been under a lot of stress so he was probably worse than usual. But he does regret it, and if you could overlook his mistake and join us, it would please me very much. And Hugo is not a bad chap, as you'll find when you get to know him better.'

Getting to kmow Hugo Cameron better was not high on her list of priorities. The last thing she wanted was to offend the kindly old man and if he thought her churlish, she was sorry. Paula dug her heels in.

'It's very kind of you to take this trouble, but . . .' She shrugged, momentarily at a loss how to make her point.

The bushy silver eyebrows rose to form an interrogatory peak above the prominent nose that was tending to beakiness in old age. Sir Iain studied her, blue eyes uncomfortably sharp. 'If there's anything else that's happened to make you upset?'

'No. No, of course not,' Paula returned hastily. There was nothing else—not unless she told him that she objected to his son eyeing her like a chunk of meat in a butcher's window, and, furious as she was, Paula wasn't about to do that. 'It's just that I have a slight headache and am not up to company.' She felt ashamed at having to trot out that tired old fib, and felt worse when it was accepted with a gracious display of tact.

'I'm sorry to hear that,' Sir Iain said simply, ambiguously perhaps, and after he'd left. Paula would have liked nothing better than to let Hugo Cameron have a piece of her mind for putting her into such a position. Just for a moment—a very fleeting one—she was almost inclined to take up the dinner invitation after all.

By the time she finally went to bed, Paula had calmed down and resisted the temptation to take a sleeping-pill. Scared to be without them, she had brought a large bottle with her but had not taken one since arriving on the island and was proud of herself for it. Why let one unsettling afternoon spoil her track record? More precisely, why let Hugo Cameron spoil it?

The nightmare brought her awake with a violent lurch of panic. Wild-eyed, Paula reared off the pillow, mouthing a voiceless scream, then fell back and lay very still with her eyes clamped shut as the sound of squealing brakes and shattering glass died away in her ears. The silence that followed was so complete she felt marooned in it; the only person left in the world. Then, very slowly, her mind started to function again and Paula became conscious of the cotton pyjamas sticking sweatily to her skin. She took a deep, shuddering breath but felt too drained to move. The nightmare always had that effect on her.

The dream never varied; it was always the last fatal drive with Mark and Stephen. They had been to stay with her parents at the farm for the weekend and, as always, Mark hadn't wanted to go but Paula had insisted because it was her parents' wedding anniversary; her two sisters were going to be there with their husbands and children—a family occasion and Paula wanted to be part of it.

She wanted Mark but more particularly, Stephen, to be part of it too. After his parents' divorce and wrangling custody case, the little boy

needed every bit of family warmth and security
he could get, but it was more than that. In a
curious way Paula needed him there. Both her
sisters were younger than Paula and between
them had three children already, whereas at
twenty-four all Paula had was a very promising
career. Having Stephen with her—and Mark too,
of course—somehow made her feel more complete, as if a void she was only subconsciously
aware of was filled. Perhaps if it hadn't been for
Stephen she might have realised sooner that
Mark wasn't the man for her.

Opposites attract. Trite, but it had been true.
Paula had taken to the quiet, unassuming solicitor
when she met him through Roger at a literary
party. Mark was light-years away from her fun-
loving friends and, for a short time at least, rather
reminded Paula of her father.

They had become engaged within months of
their meeting and only later did Paula come to
understand that under the quiet, dependable
front was a very insecure man. Mark had found her
voluble, easy-going family overwhelming, and in
some way threatening, especially her mother. The
fact that Karen Halstead was a sculptor of repute
might have even impressed the snob in Mark—if
only she hadn't been quite so 'different'.

Paula had always felt her mother deliberately
went out of her way to jolt Mark a little out of his
conventionality. And she had jolted him all right,
with her free-flowing mass of bright red hair,
colourful garb, her hit-and-miss housekeeping
and general scattiness. All the things that
enchanted her husband and that her three

daughters took in their stride Mark had found quite shocking. It was possible he had been afraid that Paula's own artistic background would turn her into someone as exotically unconventional as her mother, but whatever his reasons, he had set about changing her.

It had started with trivial things, like how she wore her hair, then her clothes, then progressed to the places they went and the people they saw: less and less of Paula's family and old friends from Art School and more and more of Mark's solicitor friends—most as conservative as himself, and with wives to match. It had been such a slow insidious process, Paula was barely aware it was happening or how much suppressed resentment she was harbouring.

On that drive back to London, Stephen had suddenly said—with that sometimes startling insight small children come out with—'Daddy doesn't like Karen, does he?'

Mark had muttered something inarticulate and the thought had seared through Paula's mind: 'No, he doesn't. And I don't like Mark.' The realisation had taken the wind out of her. A couple of miles on, she had blurted out, without any awareness that she was about to speak, 'I can't marry you, Mark. I'm sorry.' She had chosen her moment badly. The shock of her unexpected statement had swept Mark's customary caution aside and he had taken his eyes off the wet road for a few seconds too long. Weeks later, still in hospital, Paula had learnt what had happened and felt so guilty she wanted to die too.

Paula opened her eyes and stared blankly up at

the ceiling. In a moment she would get up and take a bath. She moved her right leg gingerly. It felt stiff and heavy, and she sighed in exasperation. It had happened again; every time she had the nightmare the leg seized up. It lasted four or five hours, but was a nuisance. There was nothing wrong with the leg itself any more; the doctor had explained it was all in her mind and as soon as she stopped feeling guilty over the accident the nightmares would cease and the leg would never bother her again. It sounded simple enough.

Paula got up and made herself coffee in slow motion, her mind as seized up as the leg. Everything took ages and she felt exhausted by the time she sat down with her coffee at the small table that did duty as dining and work-table. She heard the footsteps on the stony path as she took her first sip. The cup still at her lips she listened, frowning as they came closer; too impatient to be Sir Iain's; too heavy and loud for Jamie's. Paula put the cup down and waited. The peremptory rap at the door confirmed her suspicions. Pretend she was out? The thought shot through her mind. With the door unlocked? Too risky. Paula rose slowly and went to answer it.

Barely glancing at her, Hugo Cameron strode in without invitation.

'And good morning to you too, Mr Cameron,' Paula snapped cantankerously at his back.

He swung to her suddenly. The first look glanced off her, then his eyes came back and focused on her face. 'Are you all right, Paula?' The concern was sharp—and unwelcome. 'You look . . .'

'Tired, Mr Cameron?' Paula interrupted snappishly. 'Yes, I know. I didn't sleep very well.' She was piqued he had noticed she looked like a wreck—and so quickly; a man too obviously used to seeing women first thing in the morning—and his women probably looked as glamorous as they did the night before, Paula thought resentfully, remaining by the door. She was afraid to move in case he noticed the limp as well, and her pride couldn't have coped with that.

'"Mr Cameron"? Still on our high horse, are we?' he mocked, but without any real edge— almost mechanically, as if he had other things on his mind than annoying her.

'Look, if you've come to apologise about yesterday . . .' Paula started

'I haven't,' said Hugo shortly. 'It was a harmless mix-up, so if you're expecting me to grovel, you're in for a disappointment. Besides, you got your own back by reneging on dinner.'

So much for Sir Iain's version of his son's remorse. Hugo showed about as much remorse as a rock. Paula gave a tart smile. 'My mistake, but since nine-thirty in the morning is somewhat early for a social call, what exactly have you come for . . . Mr Cameron?' The icy emphasis on the address was too heavy-handed to miss.

Hugo scowled. 'The name's Hugo, why don't you use it?' he suggested irritably. 'And I came to ask if there is anything you planned to do today that can't be put off until tomorrow?'

'What do you mean?' Paula frowned uneasily, her eyes wary.

'Just what I say—have you anything lined up that can't wait?'

Paula could recognise a loaded question when she heard one. 'Why?' she demanded, ready to reject anything he was about to spring on her, but vaguely curious as to what it was going to be.

Hugo took a step towards her and Paula made a twitchy movement backwards without actually taking a step. Her hand went fluttering up to the top of her dressing-gown to make sure that the fronts were still pulled together.

'Must you stand at the door like that?' Hugo muttered testily. 'You needn't look so ready to flee—I'm not going to pounce on you.'

Her reaction had been instinctive, but silly, and Paula coloured in annoyance for her exhibition of alarmed modesty. She wasn't going to be able to walk very far today, let alone flee, but was not expecting him to pounce. She doubted the Hugo Camerons of the world ever needed to pounce.

'I want you to come to see the fort,' Hugo said, referring to one of the island's main tourist attractions. His eyes dropped from her face to her hand which seemed to have stuck to the lapels of her gown.

'Why?'

He looked up, not quite meeting her eyes. 'I thought you might be interested.' It was too nonchalant to be anything but a downright lie.

'I've seen it, but thank you for asking me,' Paula replied with precise politeness, and it did happen to be true. She had already seen the remains of the old fort. thought to have been built against Roman invaders. Sir Iain had arranged a trip for her during her first days on the island and while Paula had meant to go back for another look around, the days, weeks, had somehow fled and she hadn't found the time. However, she had no intention of making time for Hugo Cameron.

Hugo's face darkened. 'Then you can see it again,' he barked. 'I want you to come, and before you snap out another curt little "why?", the answer is the wretched boy won't go without you. You've got too much influence with him and I don't like it,' he finished in a bad-tempered mutter.

'What? You've no right to say that!' The fiery indignation welled up on the heels of her first surprise.

'Haven't I just?' Hugo countered with a return glare, then turned and walked moodily to the silk-screen curtain Paula had hung up to divide the one main room of the cottage into bedroom and living-areas. Hands in pockets, he stood staring at it with his back to her and Paula took the opportunity to edge crabwise to the chair and sit down before he turned around again.

Finished with the curtain, Hugo wandered to the tiny dresser. A pile of sketches lay on the top of it, most of them of Jamie, and Paula watched silently as he flipped through them, pausing every now and then when a particular one held his attention. He was invading her privacy but in too distracted a way for it to be deliberate. Paula checked her resentment.

'Why force the child to go if he doesn't want

to?' Still seething with indignation at his accusation, she made a superhuman attempt to be reasonable.

Hugo spun around. 'Because it will do him good, that is why,' he shot at her irritably. Paula didn't believe him and her face showed it. Hugo made a vague gesture with his hand. There was a tinge of added colour in his face. 'Miss Hunt—Louise—arranged an outing, a sort of family picnic. And you can spare me that snide, knowing look. It's not for Louise. I want Jamie to come.'

'Even if it means dragging him along against his will—and me with him?' Reasonableness fled out of the window. Paula felt her temper rising.

'It won't kill either of you. Damn it, I break my neck getting here to see the kid and he acts as if he can't stand the sight of me.'

'And you're blaming me for that?' Paula hurled at him in mock astonishment. The anger was very real.

'Calm down, I'm not blaming you for anything,' Hugo muttered peevishly. They locked eyes, Paula ready to jump down his throat, when Hugo suddenly changed tack mid-scowl. His face cleared and he smiled—quite charmingly. 'Do join us, Paula; I'd like you to come.' His eyes ranged over her face, gauging her reaction to this new approach. 'And if you've had a bad night, the fresh air will do you the world of good.'

Her face stony, Paula looked back without a flicker. What did he think she was? A naive adolescent to be bowled over by one charming smile? She wasn't about to be disarmed that easily, but she was thinking that if she refused to go, Jamie would feel she had let him down, and, after yesterday she couldn't do that to him. Her leg would probably be all right if she didn't walk around. Was it all that much to ask of her? Only smile or no smile, Hugo Cameron was not exactly asking.

He was watching her questioningly and his face would have looked quite pleasant if it hadn't been for the impatience lurking in the eyes.

Paula produced an overdone smile. 'How can I refuse when you put it so charmingly, Hugo,' she said in a deliberate little gush.

Hugo's scowl resurfaced. 'I'm glad you see it my way. If you could be at the house in an hour, I'd appreciate it.'

Even at her slow-motion pace, Paula was showered and dressed in under half an hour. She had decided on her dark woollen slacks instead of the usual jeans because they wouldn't show up her movement so much and if she was careful, the limp might escape notice completely. It was not very cold but she had put on a long jacket over her sweater just for extra camouflage.

With a fresh cup of coffee, Paula sat down at the table and used up the rest of the hour putting on make-up—something she hadn't done for a very long time. She never bothered with it on the island, and if she thought back, she hadn't bothered much before coming to the island either. When she finished, she felt she looked like a clown with smudged lipstick rubbed into her cheeks to give her colour. Who was she trying to impress anyway.

Jamie was in the hall, hovering around the

front door, nervous and wary and not the picture of someone about to enjoy an outing. When Paula walked into the living-room she realised immediately why the child had opted for hanging about the hall.

Hugo was standing edgily by the fireplace and glanced impatiently at his watch as she came in. Louise Hunt was in the armchair a little way back from the fire. You could have cut the tension with a knife. They've had a fight, Paula thought, trying not to look at either of them.

'You've met my personal assistant, Louise,' Hugo said abruptly, and Louise Hunt jerked the corners of her mouth upwards without disturbing the fixed look in her eyes.

Personal assistant—and the rest! Paula reproduced a reciprocal jerk of acknowledgement, noting with surprise that Louise didn't look as if she was planning on going anywhere, and certainly not on a picnic she had supposedly organised.

'Well, now that you're here, we can leave. Louise won't be joining us,' Hugo added tightly without offering any explanation.

And which of them had decided on that, Paula wondered with tart interest.

'I'm sure you'll manage without me,' Louise said, and the curious tinge of coyness was glaringly out of character for someone dressed with such cool sophistication in tweed and cashmere. There was no string of pearls around her neck to add to the effect but Louise showed a nice set of teeth in a pained smile. 'I have a lot of work to get through for Hugo before we head back to London tomorrow,' she said as Hugo marched out of the room, and made it sound as if her time was much too valuable to waste on picnics. The woman's suppressed huff conveyed the distinct impression that it had been Hugo who was responsible for the sudden change in plans. But London, tomorrow? Disturbed, Paula followed Hugo out of the room.

Anna was in the hall, handing over a large hamper to Hugo. Jamie presumably was already outside in the car. Paula glanced around the hall. 'What about your father?'

'What about him?' Hugo asked carelessly.

'Isn't he coming too?'

'Whatever gave you that idea?' Hugo gave a short laugh as he carried the hamper out of the front door, Anna following him with a bundle of rugs over her arm.

Paula trailed after them slowly, wincing a little as she tried not to limp, and furious that she had been inveigled into the excursion under false pretences—well, almost. Hugo hadn't said his father was coming in so many words, but he certainly had not made it clear that he wasn't. 'Family picnic,' Hugo said and Paula had jumped to the conclusion that everybody would be coming—and that meant Sir Iain as well as Louise Hunt. Under the circumstances the supercilious personal assistant would have been a welcome addition.

Paula settled back into the sleek navy suede comfort of the exotic car without a word and they started off in a strained silence. It was Hugo's expedition—let him jolly his troops, she thought sullenly, determined not to volunteer a word, and they were half way across the island before the silence was broken by Jamie piping up, 'I want to go to the toilet, please, Uncle Hugo.'

His uncle clicked his tongue in annoyance. 'Why didn't you go before we left?'

'I didn't want to go then,' the boy replied with irrefutable reason and Paula almost laughed.

Hugo pulled the car over to the side of the deserted road and stopped. 'Out you hop then.' He glanced irritably at Paula and suddenly grinned. 'If you've got to go you've got to go,' he quipped, and she returned a smile in spite of herself. But if Hugo thought she was ready to lay down arms and burst into chattiness, he had another think coming. Paula was not going to give an inch and while the temperature of the atmosphere might have gone up a degree or two, the silence continued until they reached the ruins of the fort.

The tourist attraction was not without a sprinkling of early tourists. It was Saturday, Paula remembered, and that meant the odd local family might have decided to make a day of it too. There were several cars dotted about and she noted figures trailing about the ruins and thanked her lucky stars that it was not like the day she had come with Sir Iain when they had been the only ones there. Safety in numbers? The relief seemed a bit excessive. What was she expecting Hugo to do? Try to murder her?

'What do you want to do, walk around first?' Hugo asked when he had taken the picnic paraphernalia out of the car and spread the rug a short distance from it.

'No. You and Jamie can do that. I'd rather just sit here. I don't feel like walking around for the moment.' Half-expecting to be marched around to admire the sights, Paula was pleasantly surprised when Hugo didn't press.

She watched them wander off together, side by side, but not too close. Uncle doing avuncular duty for a day before taking off to London again. For how long this time? Louise Hunt had overlooked that bit, but the point was that Hugo was going away at all, not for how long. And he had the nerve to wonder why the child treated him with such reserve—if not downright distrust.

After a while Paula pulled out the small sketch-pad she always carried about with her in her bag and started sketching the outline of the ruins of the ancient fort. She was absorbed in it when Hugo returned, alone.

'Jamie met up with a kid from one of the other parties, they seemed to be enjoying themselves.' Hugo stood looking down over her shoulder.

Paula hated people looking over her shoulder while she sketched. She snapped the pad shut.

'Don't stop,' Hugo said, but she had already slipped the sketch-pad into her bag.

Hugo lowered himself down on to the rug, and stretching out full-length, propped himself up on an elbow. 'You haven't done much lately, have you? Illustration work, I mean,' he started, conversationally.

'No,' she replied tersely, expecting the sharp brevity of the reply to put paid to further personal questions.

'My father mentioned that you haven't been well,' Hugo went on in the same conversational tone.

That was one way of putting it. 'Yes,' Paula said discouragingly, wondering how much Sir Iain had let out of the bag, but crediting him with more tact—or compassion—than to pass on to his son what he had drawn out from her about her emotional meltdown following the accident.

'And how's your current project coming along?' Hugo asked, and sounded as if he really wanted to know.

'Fine. It's almost complete,' she answered, casually. 'All I have to do is get it to the finished artwork stage, and that shouldn't take long,' she added, deliberately forthcoming, to let him know she wouldn't be staying around for much longer—if that's what he was fishing about, and she couldn't think what else it could be.

'And after that? Have you something else already lined up?'

Her sixth sense sprang into alertness. 'No,' Paula admitted cagily, on guard because Hugo's questions were not random; they were leading up to something. 'Why are you asking me all these questions?' she demanded outright, swinging her head abruptly to look him fully in the face. She put a hand to her hair to flick it back from her face and then toyed absently with a loose strand.

Hugo was studying her hair in the way Roger often did—with the same quiet mesmerised expression.

'You have very beautiful hair,' he murmured, and Paula actually blushed, dropping her hand quickly so as not to draw any more attention to her hair.

'You haven't answered my question. You're leading up to something and I want to know what it is,' she said with a surge of belligerence to cover up her embarrassment at his unexpected compliment. She was not used to compliments any more, and when they came from Hugo Cameron there had to be an ulterior motive anyway.

'Are you always so distrustful of men—or just of me?' Hugo gave an ironic smile then raised himself to a half-sitting position and said, briskly, 'Yes, you're right. I have been leading up to something. I wanted to know how you were placed because I want to offer you a job—of sorts,' he qualified cryptically.

For a crazy moment it crossed her mind that he had a publishing company tucked away in his business stable and was about to offer her a commission.

'Looking after Jamie for a few months,' Hugo said and watched her face carefully as her expression changed to project utter astonishment.

Was he serious? Paula stared at him. Hugo looked back, perfectly serious, and Paula made a sound like a cross between a snort and a disbelieving laugh. She shook her head, sending the hair flying around her face. 'No. Oh, no. You can forget that. I'm not interested. Definitely not,' she finished off the string of negatives with an abrupt laugh. 'Thanks anyway.'

Faint surprise at her vehemence showed on Hugo's face. 'But I'm not talking about a long-term commitment,' he said, painstakingly, as if she had misunderstood him. 'It would only be for a couple of months, just until . . .' Paula was shaking her head again. 'But you're fond of the child and he needs you. Jamie's become very attached to you,' Hugo persisted, his voice sharper. He studied her with a renewed intensity, his brow slightly furrowed.

Paula gave another shake of the head. 'No way.'

'And what about Jamie? Have you thought how he's going to feel if you just up and leave?'

Straight-out emotional blackmail—as low as you could get. Only Hugo Cameron had picked the wrong person. She was an expert on emotional blackmail. Hadn't Mark plied his own subtle version of it on her? 'Stephen needs this . . . Stephen needs that . . .'

'Don't try saddling your responsibilities on me! Why don't you ask yourself how Jamie is going to feel when you flit off again with Miss Whatsit tomorrow? How long is he going to have to fret for you this time?' Her voice was raised to just this side of a screech but Paula didn't care.

Taken aback, Hugo flushed. 'It's only for a couple of days,' he told her, defensively.

'Oh yes, give or take four or five weeks,' Paula hurled contemptuously, then backed away in alarm as Hugo moved towards her across the rug.

'That's it—out at last. You've been itching to throw that at me—the heartless uncle abandoning the poor child . . . that's how you've got me taped, isn't it?'

'If the cap fits,' Paula muttered under her

breath meaning Hugo to hear only not expecting his reaction. He lunged at her suddenly and gripped her shoulder hard. Paula yelped an 'ouch' and Hugo let go immediately but his eyes raged down on her alarmed face.

'Just what the hell do you think I've been doing while I've been away? Flitting, as you call it, from party to party? Chasing women? Is that what you think I've been doing while knowing the boy's here waiting for me, disturbed and upset? What do you take me for, for God's sake?' His face was contorted with jagged fury and so close Paula could have started counting the pores.

She shook her head, rattled. It sounded monstrous when said aloud, but yes, it was exactly what she thought.

Hugo pulled back, breathing hard. 'You don't like me and that's your prerogative, but you've no right to pass judgement on me, and you've no right turning the child against me.'

Paula rallied out of her fright. 'That's absurd,' she said shakily.

'Is it? I'm no fool. It's only too plain that you've influenced Jamie's attitude towards me— oh, I've no doubt you've been very subtle about it, just a word here, a word there about callous old Uncle Hugo—too busy having a good time to spare his little nephew a thought.'

'You're crazy! I would never say anything like that,' Paula protested heatedly.

'But you happen to think it's true.'

'I've never said anything against you to Jamie,' she mumbled, uncomfortably.

'How charitable of you,' Hugo mocked viciously. 'But you haven't needed to, have you? Your attitude is enough. You stared at me so furiously yesterday afternoon when you clapped eyes on me it's a wonder you didn't go cross-eyed with the effort—or turn me to stone. The boy can put two and two together, and you've made it add up to Uncle Hugo being a heartless meanie.'

Paula put a hand across her eyes, holding it there as if it would block out his contempt. She sat in silence, pricked by shame, but not convinced—not fully—that she was totally wrong about him. She took her hand away and met Hugo's eyes. 'You could have written, or telephoned, just once in a while. It would have made all the difference to him.'

Hugo's face went quite blank. 'I could have . . . what?' There was no anger in his eyes any more, instead, a gathering concern. 'What has Jamie been telling you?' he asked in a rather odd voice.

'It's a bit late to look so concerned now,' Paula returned dismissively. 'And given that we appear to think so little of each other, I wonder that you're offering me the job of looking after the child. I would have thought I'd be the last person you would choose under the circumstances.'

Hugo's mouth gave a bitter twist. 'The circumstances being what they are, I don't have much choice,' he said, almost helplessly. 'Jamie likes you, probably even loves you, and he's been through a lot. If having you around can make him happier while I sort everything out, then I'm prepared to put up with a supercilious young woman who thinks I'm the world's original cad, and makes no bones about it.' Hugo tried out a wry smile on her.

Paula looked away without response. In the distance she picked out Jamie heading towards them, a small solitary figure.

'Besides which,' Hugo continued in a curious change of voice, his eyes on her profile, 'I might find it interesting to see how quickly I can persuade her to change her opinion of me.' He lifted a hand to her averted face and ran a finger lightly down the smooth warm curve of her cheek.

Something snapped inside her at his touch, at his sardonically intimate voice—or both. Paula struck at the hand, slapping it away from her. 'Get your hands off me!' she hissed like a cat about to leap in mindless attack. 'I don't like being pawed any more than I like being ogled. Keep it for your girlfriends, I'm sure they love it—and while you're at it, why don't you ask one of them to play mummies and daddies with you!'

CHAPTER THREE

SURPRISE, or rather shock, was the first thing Hugo's eyes registered; the anger came a second later with the sweep of ugly crimson over his face. Ashen with her own fury, Paula stared him out and Hugo turned his face away, muttering something in a harsh undertone as he shifted angrily to the corner of the rug. She caught the first words, which were 'You little . . .' and suspected that what she missed was probably 'bitch'.

Paula pulled herself together with an effort as Jamie approached. Unsure of his reception, the boy stopped several feet away and whatever he saw in their faces didn't do anything to reassure him. He sized them up nervously without coming any closer.

Paula smiled shakily. 'Come and sit down, Jamie,' she invited in a hopelessly unnatural voice and Jamie edged unwillingly to a corner of the rug and sat down—as far away from both adults as possible. Then there was nothing for it but to go through the charade of having a picnic. It didn't last very long but was awful while it did.

Hugo made persistent attempts to draw the boy out, questioning him about what he had been doing with his little friend, and in the process came over like a prosecutor in full stride. Almost visibly, Jamie shrank deeper into himself until his

46

uncle couldn't get a word out of him, and while it made Paula want to yell at Hugo to leave the miserable child alone, her own efforts weren't much better when she tried to alleviate the situation by pressing Jamie to eat in a sort of bright nag.

Feeling wretched, Paula gave up, and since no one was bothering with the pretence of eating, started packing the things away. 'I think we ought to start back, don't you, Hugo?' She addressed him for the first time in Jamie's presence with sickening pleasantness.

'Yes, I suppose so,' Hugo agreed sourly without looking at her. He got to his feet and Jamie sprang up without urging.

'Well, let's be off then, shall we? Your grandfather will be wondering what's become of us,' Hugo said to Jamie, making a last-ditch stand to be hearty.

At one o'clock, when they'd barely been gone two hours? What did he take the child for? Paula stood up—too quickly, without remembering to favour her bad leg, and gave an involuntary yelp of surprised pain when she stumbled. Hugo shot out a hand and gripped her arm preventing the fall.

He glared down at her trousered legs—at both, since he had no way of telling which was causing the trouble. 'What's the matter with your leg?' he demanded, unsympathetically, digging his fingers into her arm with far more pressure than needed to support her.

'Nothing,' Paula lied shortly, then in view of the fact that she was going to limp pretty noticeably to the car under his watchful eye, added in a mutter, 'Just a pulled muscle.' She tried to move herself clear of his grip. 'It's all right, only a bit seized up, probably from sitting too long.'

'And when did this happen?' Hugo wasn't letting her go.

Avoiding his eyes, Paula shrugged. 'I don't remember; most likely walking over the rocks yesterday,' she lied.

'Yesterday?' Hugo picked up the word. 'Yesterday?' he repeated angrily. 'Then why the hell didn't you tell me this morning?' He let loose with a shout that made Jamie jump back in alarm.

'And would it have made any difference if I had?' Paula's voice rose in a retaliatory shout. 'You'd have dragged me along anyway.'

Hugo gave a raspy whistle under his breath and shook his head in disbelief. 'Boy, you really have got it down to a fine art, haven't you—making a man feel a heel.' Before Paula could retaliate, he turned sharply to Jamie who looked as if he was about to cry. 'Take the rug to the car Jamie, I'll bring the hamper in a moment. Come on, I'll help you to the car,' he said brusquely, and since his hand hadn't left her arm, it was pointless to protest. Paula allowed herself to be led carefully down the slope.

'I'm not exactly an invalid,' she snapped as Hugo eased her into the front seat like a fragile geriatric.

'Shut up,' Hugo returned evenly, but with a look in his eyes that made it clear he would have preferred to throw her bodily into the car—or possibly under it.

It was an illusion that the return trip was shorter since they went the same route, but it was definitely quicker with Hugo's foot planted hard on the accelerator for most of the way. Jamie scrambled out of the back seat the moment they pulled up in front of the house and bolted as fast as his little legs would carry him. Given half the chance, Paula would have done the same.

'You'd better let my father take a look at that leg,' Hugo said tersely, helping her out of the car as solicitously as he had put her into it—and with the same murderous look in his eyes. 'And before you trot out your objection,' he blocked off her protest as Paula opened her mouth, 'my father would like a word with you. There's something he wants to discuss. I didn't get the chance to mention it before.'

Louise Hunt lifted her eyes from the magazine on her lap. 'Goodness, back already?' she exclaimed, farcically wide-eyed with exaggerated surprise as Hugo led Paula into the living-room. Louise was sitting under the large window that gave on to the path and the drive, and Paula would have bet her last penny that the woman had been standing at it moments before.

The sherry-brown eyes did a quick summing-up of the tightly-controlled faces and were obviously pleased by what they saw; the picnic had not been a success. Louise kept the pleasure out of her voice.

'Has there been an accident?' she asked solicitously.

'No,' Hugo answered curtly as he shunted Paula across the room to the armchair by the fire. 'Where's my father?'

'In the study I presume—now that I'm out of it,' Louise said with a pointed tartness which Hugo chose to ignore. 'I finished the report you wanted,' Louise added a little less tartly.

'Good.' Hugo moved to the small round table that Sir Iain used as a drink-stand, and turned to Paula. 'What will you have? Or would you prefer tea?'

The only thing Paula really wanted was to get back to the cottage and away from the disagreeable pair as quickly as she could. 'Tea. Thank you,' she replied after a moment.

'Right.' Hugo replaced the whisky bottle on the tray without pouring himself a drink, or offering Louise one. 'I'll get Anna to make us some.'

With Hugo out of the room there was a long uncomfortable silence. Paula felt at a disadvantage with Louise out of eye's range. The woman's eyes seemed to be boring into her right ear. Paula shifted herself slightly so she could turn her head towards the window. Unabashed, Louise carried on with her silent scrutiny.

'It's a pity you weren't able to come with us. The place has rather an atmosphere about it and the ruin is very interesting,' Paula said for something to break the silence and heard herself sounding like a blurb on a third-rate tourist brochure.

Louise lifted the corners of her mouth a barely-perceptible fraction. 'I'm sure it's very interesting, but I'm not one to intrude on family outings. Hugo has had so little time with his nephew that it seemed a shame for a stranger to tag along.' She looked Paula straight in the eye.

Without a blink, Paula stared back, quite impressed that anyone could come out with such calculated rudeness. Like employer, like employee, she thought with grim satisfaction, but at least Hugo had some grounds for disliking her—or imagined he had. Louise Hunt had none ... unless ... Could the woman possibly see her as some sort of competition? A threat? The notion was too preposterous to be more than a passing thought. 'But I understand Mr Cameron will be returning in a couple of days to spend more time with Jamie,' Paula said carefully, and realised she was fishing.

Louise affected surprise with her eyebrows. 'Really?' The voice carried amused tolerance—an adult humouring a naïve child—and this time Paula flushed with annoyance.

'Hugo is a very busy man,' Louise said, painstakingly, again in that adult-to-dimwitted-child voice. 'We have a lot of things to attend to before we return to the States shortly, so it's very unlikely we'll be able to squeeze in another trip up here—much as we'd like to, of course.'

The 'we' was glaring—and deliberate, and Paula was too human not to feel an irritating flare of curiosity. It was stronger than her anger at being patronised. 'Do you always travel with Mr Cameron?' she asked, rising to the dangled bait because she couldn't help herself.

Louise's mouth curved in a genuinely pleased smile. 'Of course. I'm Hugo's personal assistant.'

'Of course,' Paula murmured drily, giving herself a mental kick, and wondered why she should feel so disturbed by something she had suspected all along. The pair could fly to the moon together for all she cared . . . only . . . Only it was plain there wasn't room for Jamie on any of their jaunts.

They had nothing to say to each other after that. Louise picked up the magazine again and started flicking through it. Paula sat staring into the fire and when Hugo returned, they had been silent for at least five minutes, so she was more than startled when Louise said, brightly, 'We'll have to continue our chat another time, Paula. I did so enjoy it.'

Hugo tossed both of them a curious look, as if he couldn't quite believe his ears either. 'My father would like a word with you now, if you don't mind, Paula.'

Paula froze him off with her eyes as he came towards her—ready to aid the invalid again—and Hugo went back to the door and held it open for her. She heard him say as the door closed behind her, 'I'd like to see that report now please Louise.' Very businesslike. Exactly like a boss talking to an employee. Keeping up a front for her benefit, Paula surmised acidly, and couldn't imagine why they bothered.

Sir Iain rose from his desk as Paula hesitated in the doorway. 'Come in, lass, and sit down. Leg hurting today?' he asked softly as Paula eased herself into the chair. She nodded briefly. 'Pulled muscle, is it?' he smiled whimsically but his eyes were serious, and Paula dropped her gaze in faint embarrassment for her childish subterfuge. Sir Iain contemplated her from his position by the window. 'It's been a while since you've had that nightmare. I think you told me the last time was about a week before leaving London.' His magnificent eyebrows jerked upwards in concentration. 'That must make it about six weeks ago.'

'Yes,' Paula said, knowing exactly to the day—or night. It had been after Roger had lashed out at her for making a mess of the illustrations, and she had gone back home and howled herself sick. That night she had had the nightmare—for the last time she had thought.

'I thought it had gone for good,' Sir Iain murmured sympathetically.

'So did I.' And had been kidding herself. Paula shrugged, and Sir Iain turned to the window. Hands locked behind his back, he stared out over the flowers, which, despite the climate, managed to grow in quite astonishing profusion inside the walled garden.

'What did you want to see me about, Sir Iain?' Paula asked, finishing her study of the back of his head ... Hugo's head; good bones must run in the family. As a sculptor, her mother would have loved to get her hands on them.

He turned back slowly. The blue eyes had lost the startling dark quality of his son's and grandson's, but they were still bright—and shrewd. 'Why didn't you tell Hugo the truth about your leg?' he asked, either ignoring her question, or so intent on his own train of thought that he had missed hearing it. Paula made an indeterminate movement of her head. 'Oh well, it doesn't matter,' Sir Iain murmured, then unexpectedly gave a soft throaty chuckle. 'Rubbed you up the wrong way, that son of mine, hasn't he?'

Paula smiled wanly at the colossal understatement. 'You wanted to see me.'

'Yes, I did. I wanted to ask if I could prevail upon you to look after Jamie.' He smiled. 'You see I . . .' he started, and that was as far as he got.

'No.' In an ungainly scramble, Paula was out of her seat, shaking her head agitatedly. Sir Iain's smile froze, then vanished. He stared at Paula as if she had taken leave of her senses, and she probably had. She was so incensed that Hugo had roped in his father to put the pressure on her to accept the job she couldn't see straight. 'No, you can't ask me to do that—it's unfair! You must know how I feel. I've explained. After Stephen . . . I . . .' She looked at him despairingly. 'Hugo had no right to ask you.'

Sir Iain recovered himself and came towards her. 'My dear, I'm sorry. I'm so sorry. I had no idea that you would feel so distressed. It was thoughtless of me. I would never have asked you to mind the lad if I'd known.' He patted her awkwardly on the shoulder. 'It's all right. I'll just postpone my trip down to London for a while, until Hugo gets back. I can go another time; it's not that important.'

Paula stared at the kindly, distressed old face, then sank down on to the chair and closed her eyes. After a moment, when she thought she had everything straightened out in her head, she snapped them open. 'Did you mean looking after Jamie . . . here? Just while you went away?' she asked, slowly.

'Yes, of course I did,' Sir Iain replied, slowly too, and they both looked at each other wordlessly while their crossed wires untangled themselves. 'I need to go to London for a week or so—to see my doctor, for one thing. No, just a check-up,' he assured her as Paula's eyes widened in concern. 'As you know, we've all been under some strain recently and it's good to keep a check on things. I wouldn't normally have considered leaving Jamie, but since you're here, I thought . . .' He finished off with a vague shrug and Paula wanted to sink through the floor.

'Heavens, I'm sorry. Of course I can look after Jamie. I'd love it, really I would. I don't know what you must think of me flying off the handle like that. I thought . . . well, I . . . I misinterpreted things.' Paula blushed, stammered and in the end just stared helplessly. It wasn't much of an explanation and how anyone would consider entrusting a child to her care after that neurotic performance, she wasn't sure.

'I think I understand, my dear,' Sir Iain said tactfully, without making clear what it was he thought he understood from her garbled explanation. 'If you're sure,' he began doubtfully.

'I'd love to help out,' Paula assured him in a burst of repentant fervour.

Sir Iain smiled. 'In that case I can leave as planned. Hugo has suggested flying, instead of driving. He thinks the drive might be a bit too much for me, and I have to agree. He'll take the car back with him next time. We intended to leave tomorrow morning but if that doesn't suit you, we can put it off a day or two.'

'Tomorrow's fine, really it is.' Then something occurred to her and Paula frowned. 'Jamie . . . does he know about you leaving?'

Sir Iain nodded. 'Yes, I've already explained to him—and Hugo has too—or tried to. I know the lad takes Hugo's absences very badly; it's understandable after the loss of his parents, but it doesn't make things any easier for Hugo. Try as he might, it seems that nothing but Hugo's actual presence will do.'

A peculiar doubt sprang into Paula's mind. She said without emphasis, 'Hugo does keep in touch though, doesn't he, when he's away?'

'Yes, of course he does—all the time,' Sir Iain replied quickly. He looked at her worriedly—the same way Hugo had looked earlier. 'Has Jamie been saying that he doesn't?' he asked, his voice unintentionally sharp.

'No, he's never said that,' Paula said hurriedly and Sir Iain's face cleared, but he sighed heavily. 'Sometimes I've wondered whether Hugo's constant phone calls and letters haven't made it worse for the child; when you're six years old and been through what Jamie's been through, a disembodied voice on the other end of the telephone can't really allay all the terrors and anxieties, can it?' he smiled sadly, and made a helpless gesture with his hands. 'But what can you do?'

Nothing. But she could have asked—five weeks ago. One direct question to Sir Iain or Anna; or Jamie himself, that's all it would have taken to find out how things really stood. Instead she had—and with satisfaction at that—built up her own misguided picture of a callous, uncaring man. And just how much had her po-faced attitude towards 'Uncle Hugo' rubbed off on the child? She had never deliberately said anything against the man, but perhaps Hugo was right; perhaps she hadn't needed to state her disapproval for the child to pick it up and become more confused than he already was.

She should have searched Hugo out and apologised straight away. She had meant to, but he had still been closeted in the living-room with Louise and Paula hadn't been able to face him. And that made her feel worse—a coward, on top of a shrew.

She took a sleeping-pill that night, and took it early because she couldn't stand the prospect of hours of emotional turmoil trying to come to terms with herself, trying to rationalise her hysterical attacks, when she knew they didn't lend themselves to any rationalisation. Flying off the handle at Hugo had been bad enough; turning on Sir Iain like a demented fishwife was unpardonable, however she had misinterpreted his request to mind the child.

What price all her back-patting and self-congratulations now? Paula asked herself miserably, staring out through the window at the fading light as she lay in bed waiting for the pill to do its job. She might have her work under control but if the crazy outbursts were anything to go by, she was still a very long way from sorting out the mess inside her head, and she didn't know where to start.

At bottom, it seemed that the problem was still

her tangled feelings of guilt about Stephen, and not wanting to get involved with another child was understandable. Her over-reaction both with Hugo and Sir Iain had been a self-protective measure, but was that all there was to it? That still did not explain why she had been so outraged when Hugo had made his pass. A pass, that's all it had been, Paula reminded herself; other men had made passes before and she had never reacted with such wild-eyed outrage. But then, she had never felt so . . . threatened.

In the morning Paula felt thick-headed and listless—the usual side-effect of the sleeping-pill, but infinitely preferable to yet another re-run of the nightmare. She got herself moving with an effort, and having promised to be with Jamie when the party left for the airport, was at the house and holding the child's hand as the sedan drove away. Sir Iain was in the front seat with Neil; Hugo in the back with a very pleased-looking Louise Hunt.

Hugo's last words had been 'see you both in a few days.' He had his arm around Jamie's shoulder as he said them but had been looking directly into Paula's eyes.

'I'm sure Jamie will be looking forward to that,' Paula had replied, intending to sound casual, and had come across surly and dis-believing, and that was not the way she had meant to sound, but her embarrassment at not having yet apologised to him had got in the way. The angry flash in Hugo's eyes told her he simply thought she didn't believe him.

At the end of the day, Anna took the call from

London, Paula was there when Jamie spoke to his grandfather and then to Hugo. Paula didn't ask him about the call and two minutes later Jamie was acting as if he hadn't spoken to his uncle at all. It was grandfather this and grandfather that. So that's how it had been, Paula thought with a renewed stab of guilt that she hadn't forced herself to apologise to Hugo before he had left.

Anna's day off fell on the fourth day after Hugo's departure. The old lady usually spent the day and night with her daughter in the island's main town and it was only after she was gone that Paula became aware how much difference Anna's voluble presence had made. Without it, the house seemed unnaturally silent. She and Jamie stayed by the fire in the living-room all day. The wind was working itself up into a passable imitation of a gale, but even without it they probably would have remained in the house since both of them seemed to have ground to a sort of apathetic halt and neither wanted to do anything.

Paula felt on edge and as the evening drew on the edginess increased. She blamed it on the wind and told herself not to be stupid as she pottered about the large comfortable kitchen putting together the meal Anna had prepared for them before leaving. Jamie seemed edgy too. There had been no call from Hugo that day and neither of them referred to the fact. Jamie had withdrawn into himself and was silent while she got him ready for bed. When she tucked him in, he looked at her steadily, a too-old depth in his eyes. 'I'm a nuisance, aren't I?' he said expressionlessly.

Paula stared at him in horror. 'No, Jamie!

Where in heaven's name did you get an idea like that?'

'Miss Hunt told me,' he replied with an adult casualness. 'I don't care. I hate everybody. I don't care if Uncle Hugo doesn't come back.'

In the murderous fury that shot through her, Paula would have cheerfully strangled the woman with her bare hands. 'Your uncle will be back, Jamie,' she said harshly. 'He told you he will and you must believe him.'

Jamie turned his face to the wall and Paula sat helpless and silent until the smooth rise and fall of his shoulders told her he was asleep. Back in the kitchen, she hurled the few dishes through some hot water in the sink with a savageness that would have given Anna a seizure, and came to a decision. When Hugo returned, she would tell him she would accept his job of looking after Jamie; she didn't have a choice any more; the child needed her, badly.

Later, in the bath, Paula was still thinking about it, and had swung from the first initial doubt to almost light-headed cheerfulness. A couple of months—just to tide Jamie over his patch of insecurity, and help Hugo out at the same time. After misjudging him as she had, she owed him at least that.

In spite of the heavy woollen dressing-gown, Paula shivered when she came out of the warm, steamy bathroom. The wind had not let up once, only now it sounded as if it had joined forces with a torrential downpour of rain and developed into one of those full-scale storms that hit the island without any warning. Securely tucked up in her cosy cottage, she loved listening to them; alone in a very large house with only a sleeping child, the storm gave her the creeps. The lights were on all over the house but they didn't allay the nervousness that had set in. Paula shivered again and hurried into Jamie's room to check on the child.

He was tossing restlessly, the bedclothes pushed halfway down the bed, and whimpered softly as she drew the covers over him. After a moment's hesitation, Paula climbed on to the bed and lay alongside the small restless body, placing an arm over it. The warmth of it seemed to quieten him; the breathing became more regular again and Jamie stopped tossing. Paula closed her own eyes.

Some time later she jerked awake, rearing into a sitting position. Utterly disorientated, it took her a few moments to realise that the warm shape beside her was Jamie. Her watch was in the guest-room and Paula had no idea how long she had been asleep; it might have been minutes or hours. The light was on in the room—they were still on all over the house, yet she felt alarmed, certain that some sound had woken her. As she strained her ears against the wind and rain lashing at the window, very definite sounds carried into the room—sounds of someone in the house, coming up the stairs, Her heart stopped, then the next second started racing madly.

Paula froze into rigidity, and, even half-senseless with fright, was vaguely conscious that her tension had penetrated Jamie's sleep. He shifted uneasily against her while she couldn't have moved to save her life. Eyes dilated like a terrified child's, she waited and when the figure came through the doorway the only reason she didn't scream was she couldn't find her voice.

Her eyes told her the man was Hugo Cameron, but the message was a long time reaching her brain. When she came out of her freeze, Hugo was bending over her, calming her. 'It's okay Paula, it's okay. It's me—Hugo.' His voice was soft, gruff—shocked. 'For God's sake don't stare at me like that. I didn't mean to frighten you. The lights were on. I thought you were awake, I called out.'

She let the trapped air out of her lungs in short shallow gasps and turned on him—savagely. 'Of all the damn stupid things to do! What do you mean by sneaking up on me like that?' she hissed through lips that wouldn't stop quivering. Her shoulders still shook violently under his arm.

Hugo tightened his hold. 'I didn't sneak.' He cut off his hiss midway because Jamie was stirring. They both stared down at him, waiting for him to be still again. Paula's own shaking was subsiding. She made a sharp, angry movement with her shoulder. 'I'm all right now.'

Taking the hint, Hugo removed his arm and very carefully Paula eased herself away from Jamie's body and out of the bed. She rammed her feet into her slippers, then leant over and tucked the blanket more securely around Jamie's shoulders. As she straightened up she met Hugo's eyes, watching her with an unfamiliar intensity, and something disconcerting mingling with the concern in them. Instinctively, her hands reached for the lapels of her dressing-gown, yanking them together. Her nerves must still have been shot, because she blushed suddenly for no reason at all. 'It was an idiotic thing to do,' she snapped at him in a undertone to cover her momentary confusion.

Outside the door, Hugo tried putting his arm around her again, then, on second thoughts, took it off smartly. 'Come downstairs; you need a drink. I gave you a bad fright. I'm sorry,' he said with a small, contrite smile.

Terrified out of her wits, she couldn't deny she needed the drink. Paula nodded. 'I'll get dressed,' she said brusquely.

Hugo made an impatient gesture with his hand. 'There's no need for that. The fire's still going in the living-room.' He flicked an eye over the dressing-gown. 'You'll be warm enough as you are.'

It was not the cold Paula was thinking about. She felt uncomfortable and at a disadvantage in the dressing-gown—why, she couldn't have said; it would have been as easy to see through a lead door as its weighty thickness. She went downstairs with him as she was.

CHAPTER FOUR

SHE stood by the fire holding her hands down to it, feeling the warmth start at her fingertips and seep slowly through her. When Hugo handed her the whisky Paula took it without a word; the glass felt cold and she curved her hands around it, bringing it closer to the fire.

'Drink it,' Hugo ordered and must have realised how sharp that sounded, because he added, cajolingly, 'Drink it up, Paula, you need it. I'll make you a cup of tea later, if you like,' he offered as an afterthought, and sounded . . . kind.

Granted she had had a bad fright, but he didn't have to turn around and treat her like a recalcitrant invalid to be humoured and bullied into taking her medicine. Paula took a small sip.

'Good girl,' Hugo encouraged approvingly in a voice she had used herself with Jamie, and Paula made a mental note to avoid using it with the child in future. She moved away from him and sat down in the armchair at the other end of the fireplace and took another sip of the whisky, swirling the fiery liquid around her mouth before swallowing it. 'How did you get here?' she asked, suddenly curious. The clock on the mantelpiece showed nine-thirty but it was long past the last ferry or plane from the mainland.

'Flew in. The plane was delayed in Glasgow for ages because of the weather, otherwise I would have been here hours ago,' Hugo explained.

They were about eight miles from the town and the airport. Paula remembered noticing a heavy black mac tossed across the back of a chair in the hall. She frowned at Hugo's shoes. They looked dampish but his dark business suit was dry. 'But how did you get . . . here?'

Hugo gave an abrupt laugh. 'I didn't walk, if that's what you're thinking. I rang up Calum from the airport. The good chap came away from his fireplace and got out his old monstrosity of a cab. We do have a few facilities on the island, you know.' Hugo smiled, teasingly, and Paula was quite aware that he was going all out to relax her. And well might he after scaring her half to death.

They remained silent for a minute or two, listening to the sounds of the storm outside, and the room seemed mellower . . . cosier, just for having another person in it. She thought of Jamie sleeping peacefully upstairs and felt vaguely happy for him, visualising the child's relief when he woke and found that Uncle Hugo had kept his promise and come back after all. Paula lifted her eyes from the glass on her lap.

'I . . . we . . . didn't expect you back.' Back tonight, she had meant, and started quickly to clarify. 'What I meant was . . .'

'Is that so?' Hugo countered tightly without letting her finish. His features were already seized up into a scowl and the hazy façade of companionableness was gone in a flash.

Irrationally angry he had taken her up the wrong way, and conscience just a little pricked by the shadow of doubt that had stayed willy-nilly in her mind, Paula swung blindly into attack. 'And how long is Jamie going to have you around this time?' she sniped.

Hugo grimaced then gave a surly shrug. 'Two weeks—longer, if I can manage it,' he muttered, and she was a little surprised he had chosen to answer without a retaliatory snipe.

'And then?' She really wanted to know, but couldn't do anything about the acid in her voice.

'And then.' Hugo took an angry step towards her and Paula backed into her chair, faintly alarmed by the look on his face. 'And then, since you're so interested in my activities, I'm going back to the States to try and sort out the rest of the mess that my brother left behind him.' Two paces from her, Hugo stopped and turned to the fire. He put both hands on the high mantelpiece and stared down into the flames. With his head down, and body in slump, he did not look arrogant, angry or any of the other derogatory adjectives Paula associated with him. Hugo looked ... worn out, and she felt a jab of guilt that she was sitting about needling him when he should have been in bed getting some rest.

'Look, I didn't mean to sound like that ... I ...' The 'I'm sorry' stayed stranded in her throat.

Hugo turned to her slowly and studied her contemplatively, as if he was trying to make up his mind about her, or about something. 'You may not know it,' he began without any anger, or indeed any emotion at all in his voice, 'but my brother, Jamie's father, was my business partner and there are legalities to iron out that will take months. He was in America looking after that side of the business, and he made a right royal mess of it.'

'You don't have to tell me, it's not my business,' Paula cut in hastily.

'The best that can be said of James's business dealings,' Hugo went on as if she had not spoken, 'was that he was . . . careless. I could use other words, and some people do, words like incompetent, and a great deal worse. There's talk of embezzlement.' His mouth gave a sour twist at the horror on her face. 'Shareholders over there are queuing around for blocks to sue the pants off me, and it will take me months to get some sort of order into the mess—even if I work twenty-four hours a day.' He looked at her bleakly, as if he was seeing a picture of those unpleasant months in front of him. 'It hasn't been easy on any of us . . . my father . . .'

'It's not my business,' Paula interrupted again, wanting him to stop. She felt more shaken by what she was seeing than hearing; Hugo with his guard down, unexpectedly vulnerable. Behind the bitter flippancy as he spoke of his brother, she could detect the hurt and grief in his voice.

'You seem to have made it your business,' Hugo accused wearily. 'You've jumped to your conclusions and made your judgments about me.'

Paula felt gutted by shame. 'I was wrong. I'm sorry,' she said in a small voice and caught him by surprise. The look he gave her was not quite of suspicion, but close. 'I did . . . jump to

conclusions, about you and Jamie. I had no right.
I'm sorry.' She offered the apology she should
have made days ago.

After a very long silence Hugo gave a quick
jerky nod. He didn't ask how she had come to
realise her mistake, and didn't appear at all
interested. He said gruffly, 'The boy's been
through a rough patch.'

And so have you, Paula suddenly thought and
felt a surge of compassion, and of helplessness.
'I'm sorry about your brother.' It sounded facile,
but there was no other way of offering her
compassion, and she couldn't be sure that Hugo
would want it from her.

Hugo pressed his eyes shut, face contorted as if
with pain. 'I loved him,' he burst out angrily, in
spite of himself, Paula thought, then opening his
eyes, looked at her with a sort of bewildered
bleakness she had sometimes seen in Jamie's eyes.
Seeing it in the man caught her off guard.
Another moment and she would have given in to
the instinct that made her want to reach out and
fold him in her arms to comfort him.

Disconcerted by the momentary intensity of
her feelings, Paula said quickly, 'There's something I wanted to tell you. I've thought over your
offer and I've decided to accept.' She stopped.
Hugo was looking blank and she hurried on,
flushing a little. 'Looking after Jamie for you. I'm
prepared to do it, just for a couple of months of
course, but it should help you out.' She finished
off her slightly disjointed speech with a self-
conscious smile.

At the back of her mind Paula supposed she must

have been expecting Hugo would be pleased
—perhaps not rapturously, but she was not
expecting that tight closed-up expression that
made him look as if he didn't know what she was
talking about—or didn't want to know. 'If the offer
still stands, that is,' she put in with a tinge of
huffiness because all at once she felt embarrassed.

'It doesn't,' he told her, quite abruptly with a
shake of the head, and her first reaction was an
odd sensation of disappointment.

'Why not?'

Hugo shrugged, uncomfortably. Paula stared
puzzled.

'You've found someone else.' She plucked the
only logical explanation out of the air.

'No, I haven't,' Hugo muttered.

'But if you haven't found anyone else, then
why?' Paula heard herself protesting heatedly and
shut up, overcome with confusion.

'Let's just say I've changed my mind as well.'
Hugo cocked his head to one side and looked at
her curiously. 'Don't tell me you're disappointed?' he asked with a hint of a wry smile.

Caught out, the red seared into her face. 'Don't
be ridiculous. I didn't want the job in the first
place.' That was not the way she was acting. She
was behaving with all the hurt and resentment of
having a prize job snatched away from her. 'I was
only thinking of Jamie,' she explained pointedly.
'He's been feeling so terribly insecure and I
thought . . .'

'That you would overcome your dislike of me
for the child's sake?' Hugo prompted, a faint
sarcastic edge in his voice.

'Something like that, yes,' Paula agreed shakily, wondering how on earth she had thought the man needed her help, how he had brought out that strange intense concern in her moments ago.

'Then you'll no doubt be relieved that I'm not taking you up on it. Thank you for the offer,' Hugo added with an ironic courtesy that made Paula feel she had just propositioned him and been turned down flat. It was a very galling feeling.

'What I've decided,' Hugo started again conversationally, without the ironic overtones, 'is that Jamie will stay on here with my father until I get back from the States, then I'll take him down to London with me.'

Where half a dozen Louise Hunts would fall over themselves racing to the aid of the guardian in distress, and none of them would give a damn about the child. Paula sprang to her feet. 'That's your business. You don't have to explain anything to me,' she said, hackles on end, and quite appalled she was behaving so irrationally. She looked about for somewhere to slam down her glass before it dropped out of her shaking hand.

Hugo moved to her side and plucked the glass from her fingers. He put it on the mantelpiece beside his own. 'Look here, Paula, I didn't mean to make you angry,' he began testily. 'It was very kind of you to reconsider my request, and I appreciate it,' he said stiffly. 'It's just not necessary any more, that's all. I . . . well . . .' he shrugged, 'there are reasons.'

The addition was curiously evasive, and about to try and push past him, Paula picked up the curious tone of voice and stopped. She stared at him, frowning. What reasons? What could have happened in the space of less than a week for Hugo to change his mind and not want her?

And it came to her ... the slow trickle of realisation that some time during the last couple of days Sir Iain must have filled Hugo in about her. And why not? She had not consulted the retired doctor as a patient, she had simply confided in him as a friend and it hadn't occurred to her to bind him to secrecy. So naturally, he would have told Hugo about Mark and Stephen, the accident, and her terrible guilt; probably her nightmares too. No wonder Hugo had changed his mind. With that sort of emotionally messy background she'd hardly be anybody's choice for looking after a child. She should have realised Hugo would find out about her sooner or later.

'I quite understand,' Paula said tightly, all at once feeling as exposed and as vulnerable as Hugo had looked a short while ago when he had been talking about his brother. She swerved her eyes away from his baffled face and tried to move past him again.

Hugo caught her roughly by the arm. 'What is it, Paula? What in heaven's name have I said? I didn't mean to upset you.'

Paula bit hard into her bottom lip which had started to quiver. She shook her head miserably as Hugo stared at her, completely at a loss. Then unexpectedly, as if it was the only thing he could think of, he wrapped his arms around her and

pulling her to him, held her so tightly Paula
could not have moved even if she'd wanted to.
Calmed into a vague numbness, she didn't react
when Hugo put a hand under her chin and lifted
her face. She closed her eyes and stayed
motionless as his mouth brushed her lips lightly
in a soft kiss that might have meant 'I'm sorry'—
or nothing at all.

The kiss would have ended on the vaguely
comforting, almost impassive note, if her lips
hadn't parted suddenly in response—a pleading
response that caught Hugo off-guard in the act of
pulling his mouth away. Paula felt his momentary
surprise before his lips resumed the kiss with
increased pressure. Easing his hands caressingly
into her hair, Hugo tilted her head back gently to
give his mouth more leverage and Paula slackened
yieldingly against him on a wave of warm,
mindless desire.

The part of her brain that was standing back,
coldly looking on, told her she was doing the
kissing now, and that the intensity and urgency
were hers; Hugo was not holding back but he was
allowing her all the initiative.

And she took it, urged on by an instinctive
hunger for his mouth, the pressure of his body.
Hugo's hands slid down the curve of her back,
holding her hard against himself while her own
hands reached around his neck, twining into his
hair and kneading agitatedly into his shoulders as
Paula abandoned herself to satisfying the wild
surge of longing that was carrying the kiss out of
control.

Out of whose control? The lips moving down

the arch of her throat knew exactly what they were doing. Paula pulled away in a breathless daze. With their arms still locked around each other she looked into Hugo's eyes and read the desire in them, and the need. Or was it her own eyes reflected back at her? There was a question too, in his dark blue depths: Hugo was virtually asking her where she wanted to go from here.

The image that flooded her mind told her where she wanted to go. The picture was so erotic—and graphic—it made Paula catch back a gasp of shock, and brought a wave of heat into her cheeks. She wasn't conscious she had moved closer against him but was aware she had started to tremble. Hugo tightened his arms around her. His eyes hadn't left her face. The question was still in them and every nerve in her body throbbed her answer for her in the silence that seemed to be extending into eons.

Then suddenly, Paula shook her head and took her hands away from Hugo's neck. Abruptly, he unclasped his arms from her back; the expression in his eyes changed to having no expression at all.

'No, of course not,' he said in a brusque undertone—more to himself than to her, and made no move to stop her as Paula fled the room.

Another kiss, that's all it would have taken to sweep her back into that exquisite mindlessness and the last of her reservations would have melted into thin air. A man of Hugo's experience must have known that, and yet he had let her walk away.

Hunched up on the bed in the guest-room, her hands wrapped around her knees, Paula told

herself she should be feeling grateful instead of—
resentful, there was no other word for it. There
was no question she had wanted Hugo to make
love to her—for all the wrong reasons. Love
hadn't come into it; she did not love him; it was
simply a momentary blend of sexual attraction
and need of comforting and she had been ready to
leap into bed with a man she barely knew—had
wanted to, and hang the consequences.

Is that how one-night stands came about? She
had often been curious about women who did that
sort of thing, and now she had nearly done it
herself—was even regretting that she hadn't.

But how did those women—'easy women', she
still thought of them as—feel the next morning?
Did they wake up hating themselves? And how
would she have felt, Paula wondered, when she
had never before said 'yes' to a man in her life—
even a man she thought she had loved—in the
beginning at any rate.

Mark had tried to make love to her once, early
in their relationship, and all this time later, the
recollection of her reaction still made Paula
cringe. She had turned to stone, appalled by the
feel of his hand on her breast, and that was as far
as they had got before she started bleating
horrified 'nos'. It had been embarrassing and
humiliating for both of them and after that first
abortive attempt, Mark had never tried again.

And that in itself was curious. Had he been
angry . . . frustrated, during their long, peculiarly
platonic engagement, or had it never really
mattered to him, with his main concern being to
acquire a stepmother for Stephen?

Somewhere quite early along the line, Paula had sensed that that was the role in store for her, and had accepted it—without resentment, she thought. It seemed to tie in with her own need for a family, but perhaps deep down it had not been what she needed or wanted. Perhaps it had been the reason she had felt so cold towards Mark, unconsciously frozen up with resentment that he hadn't wanted her for herself.

And had she been sexually frustrated all that time without realising it . . .? That would go some way in explaining her unpredictable response to Hugo, and why her body had sent out its crazy urgent messages. Only her mind was another matter; she had come out a psychological mess after her relationship with Mark, not knowing who she was nor what she wanted any more; but jumping into bed with Hugo Cameron was unlikely to have solved that for her.

Paula drifted off into an uneasy sleep. She woke several times during the night feeling cold, but some time after the dismal grey streaks of dawn, fell into a heavy doze and it was late when she came out of it. She got up feeling she hadn't slept at all and flung herself into her dressing-gown as the soft tap sounded on the door. 'Yes?' Paula called, edgily, because it didn't sound like Jamie.

Hugo put his head around the door. His hair was still damp from a shower and his face had the pinkish smoothness that comes just after a shave.

'Hello, you're up,' he said lightly. 'I just wanted to let you know Jamie is in my bed, in case you looked in on him. I didn't want you to worry.'

'Oh,' Paula said, looking into his face rather fixedly so her eyes wouldn't stray down to the damp curling hair visible between the fronts of his heavy black towelling robe.

Hugo smiled, warily. 'He woke during the night and I took him into my room so he wouldn't disturb you,' he explained.

'Yes. I see. Thank you.' Paula produced the words in stiff jerks.

Hugo wanted to say more; she could see that. He stood in the doorway, hesitating, not coming nor going. In the end, he gave another tentative smile and said with jarring heartiness, 'Well, I'll see you down at breakfast when you're ready.'

She had been wondering how they would act towards each other in the morning; Hugo had given her the cue—act as if nothing had happened. 'Yes, fine. I'll be down soon,' Paula said, breezily.

Hugo was in the kitchen when she came downstairs. Unobserved, Paula stood in the doorway taking in the curiously domestic scene. Dressed in faded jeans and a well-worn sweater, Hugo looked completely at home in Anna's comfortable territory—as if making breakfast with a six-year-old dogging his heels was something he did every day of the week.

Appearances were deceptive; the strong whiff of burnt toast told the real story. Hugo suddenly swung from the frying-pan on the stove to the toaster on the workbench. 'Damn it, Jamie, I told you to watch that,' he chided, lifting out the charred bread and hurling it into the kitchen bin.

To Paula's surprise, Jamie laughed. 'Sorry,

Uncle Hugo,' he chirped back cheerfully, not the least upset by his uncle's rebuke, and following on Hugo's heels like an excited puppy. There was no sign of the withdrawn little boy of the last couple of days. Paula couldn't help wondering what magic uncle had managed to work on nephew during the early hours of the morning when they were companionably tucked up in bed together.

She came into the room. 'Hello Jamie,' she smiled at the child.

'Uncle Hugo is making breakfast,' Jamie beamed and Hugo laughed, giving the boy's head an affectionate ruffle.

'Incredible optimist, this child. We could do with some help, couldn't we, Jamie?'

'Yes,' Jamie agreed, grinning.

Easier with the child around to take the edge off the strain between the adults. It had been like that with Stephen too, Paula remembered, that same artificial air of cosiness. The memory set off faint warning bells inside her head as they sat around the table.

'We're like a family, aren't we?' Munching on his toast, Jamie tossed in the ingenuous question without directing it at either of them.

After the slightest pause, Paula went on spreading marmalade on her toast with very intense concentration.

'Yes, we are, aren't we?' Hugo agreed, rather too airily after the long silence.

Paula looked up with no expression on her face, met Jamie's eyes, and forced out a thin smile. 'If you've finished your breakfast Jamie,

I'll start clearing away. I'm sure you and your uncle have a lot of things planned for today and you'll want to get started as soon as possible.'

'Oh, we're in no hurry,' Hugo said blandly, pouring himself another cup of tea. 'I'll be here long enough for us to do all the things we want.' He cast an eye towards the window. 'Looks like we'll be staying inside today, the weather is too dismal for anything else. We might try a spot of chess.'

'Uncle Hugo can teach you chess too, Paula,' Jamie offered, pathetically anxious to include her in their activities.

Paula's lips curved mechanically. 'That would have been nice,' she fibbed briskly, 'but I'm afraid I'll be too busy for that today. I need to pack because I'm leaving for London tomorrow.' She wasn't looking at Hugo as she said it, but was immediately aware that he had tensed. Jamie stared at her uncomprehendingly. It was not the way she would have chosen to break the news to the child, but until she announced it, the idea had not crossed her mind—her conscious mind that is; it must have been lurking in her sub-conscious from the moment she fled the living-room last night. Paula said hurriedly, 'You can come down to the cottage later, Jamie, and we'll have a chat there.'

'No,' Jamie answered stonily and turned away from her with a jerk of his shoulder that looked a direct copy of one of his uncle's angry shrugs.

'I think you should go upstairs and make your bed, Jamie—I'll give you a call when I've got the chess set out.' Hugo came into the conversation at last.

Just for a moment, Jamie looked as if he was going to protest, then he rose from the table and marched huffishly out of the room.

Hugo stayed silent, watching Jamie disappear through the doorway, waiting to make sure the boy was out of earshot before he swung back to her. 'What the hell did you have to go and do that for?' he barked.

Paula reproduced Jamie's angry shrug. 'I'm leaving tomorrow,' she repeated.

'Over my dead body.'

'If that's the way you want it.' Paula squeezed out a pinched smile.

Hugo gave a raspy laugh. 'Oh, no, you're not leaving. You'll stay put. I'm not having Jamie upset just because you're miffed with me.'

Miffed? She was a little more than miffed—and it wasn't with Hugo. She was angry with herself for her own vulnerability to him, and downright scared if it came to that. 'I'm not miffed. I have things to attend to in London and need to get down there as soon as possible,' Paula said, reasonably.

Hugo contemplated her through his scowl for some moments. 'Look, about last night . . .' he began in a different tone of voice.

'Last night has got nothing to do with anything,' Paula cut him off, and rose to her feet.

Hugo gave a mocking smile. 'If you say so.' Then as Paula reached for Jamie's plate to take to the sink, Hugo leant across the table and caught her wrist, holding her hand down to the table. Paula winced slightly, stared down at him with hostile eyes, but made no attempt to pull her hand free.

'Last night happened,' Hugo said crisply, 'but it won't happen again. I'm not going to make any advances, so unless you want to make them to me—and mean them, I might add—we can forget the whole thing and you can stop acting as if I'd subjected you to a fate worse than death. You might remember that I didn't. We happen to have kissed. It was no big deal so let's leave it at that; there's no need to make a production out of it.'

Win some, lose some, that was his attitude, and it was a safe bet that Hugo Cameron won more than he lost, and that he didn't spend fruitless hours agonising about the whys and wherefores of every passionate encounter. Paula yanked at her hand. 'Let me go,' she snapped, stung by humiliation.

'Not before you tell me you're staying,' Hugo replied with an infuriating calmness, his fingers not giving an inch.

'I can't. I've arranged to see my publisher.' The unpremediated lie popped out to her rescue. Hugo released her wrist and Paula started rubbing at where his fingers had clamped the flesh.

'Really? I didn't know that,' Hugo said with sharp interest.

'Yes. It's been arranged for a while. I've promised to bring my illustrations. He wants to have a look at them.' Paula elaborated on the lie.

'But I thought you hadn't finished them yet.' Hugo's voice held a note of polite surprise.

'They're not quite finished,' Paula conceded, trying to remember how much she had told him at the picnic, 'but they're ready enough to be looked at.'

'Oh, I see. Your publisher is waiting on them now?'

This was all much easier than Paula expected. 'Yes, that's right. I'll be seeing him in a couple of days' time.'

'How many publishers are you working for?' Hugo asked lightly.

Paula looked at him perplexed, then gave a small laugh. 'Just the one—and that's enough.'

'Then who are you going to be seeing in London when Roger Harris is up here on the island?' Hugo sprang the question on her without any change in the blandness of his voice.

'What are you talking about?' Paula frowned, momentarily stumped.

Hugo bared his teeth snidely. 'Roger Harris had lunch with my father the other day and I gather they've arranged that he'll be coming up shortly. I understand your publisher has decided he needs to see you rather urgently. Do you think he's forgotten about your apointment with him in London?' Hugo asked with wide-eyed innocence, and Paula looked at him in dislike for letting her trip along with her lie for so long.

'That was a rotten thing to do.'

Hugo leaned back in his chair. 'Yes, wasn't it?' he agreed smugly. 'So what's your next excuse?'

CHAPTER FIVE

ANNA said, and it seemed like for the twentieth time in the last three days, 'The child's really come out of himself, Miss Paula; it's a joy to see him now; he feels he belongs again.' She put the coffee pot on the side-table within reach of the card-table set up near the fireplace, and turned to Paula with a quite remarkable display of teeth for someone who looked too old to have any. 'It's having you and Mr Hugo around that's doing it.' She nodded, sagely, a pleased wiry little gnome.

Busy stacking up the cards, Paula returned a perfunctory smile of acknowledgment with a lot of suppressed exasperation behind it. 'Yes, I suppose so,' she felt obliged to murmur, wishing the old lady would let up ramming her point home. Paula was only too aware of the change in Jamie—and the reason for it. She was pleased about the change; the reason worried her. They were playing at 'happy families' and it was not going to last forever. And what was going to happen to Jamie's sense of security when it was all over, when she left, when Hugo left again?

Then at the door, Anna said with all the subtlety of a sledgehammer, 'You can never tell what Fate has in store for the three of you, you get on so well.' She grinned into Paula's startled face.

Paula gave a sudden laugh. 'You're incorrigible,

Anna,' she said, returning to the cards as Anna disappeared out of the door, but wasn't nearly as amused by the old lady's innuendo as she made out.

True; she and Hugo had got on surprisingly well, all things considered. The embarrassing episode in the living-room on the night of his return might never have happened—except that Paula couldn't get it out of her mind, and every now and then when she turned suddenly and found Hugo watching her, she knew from something in his expression that he hadn't forgotten it either.

They never referred to it, but there was an undercurrent of tension between them nevertheless. Hugo had never so much as touched her again. He had gone out of his way to be friendly, pleasant and amusing, and downright devious too, never insisting she take part in the activities he had planned with Jamie, just turning up at the cottage with Jamie in tow, all ready for the walk or drive, or the trip into town. The child took it for granted she was coming too, and when it came to the crunch, Paula couldn't refuse.

In the same way, she had been manoeuvred into joining them for the evening meal, and often a game of cards before Hugo took the child to bed. But very soon after, Hugo would walk her back to the cottage; they took great care never to be alone together for too long—but Anna would have missed that bit, just as she missed the tension in their attitude towards each other. The old lady saw only what she wanted to see, and on the surface, at least, they must have presented a very cosy picture. Appearances being what they were, was it any wonder Anna was whizzing through the air jumping to her outlandish conclusions?

And was the exasperating old lady all that far off the mark? The uneasy thought brought Paula's hand to a sudden standstill in the middle of clearing the card table. Could Hugo be playing his own little game with her, putting her through some sort of probationary exercise to test her suitability for looking after Jamie? Now that she thought about it, why else would he have pressured her into staying. She was 'no big deal' in the romance stakes—he had practically told her so, and he hadn't made another advance, just as he promised. But he did appear to want her around, and Jamie was the obvious reason. She was surprised that it hadn't occurred to her before.

Paula poured herself a cup of coffee then settled into the armchair and waited impatiently for Hugo to return downstairs. 'Listen,' she plunged in, the moment he entered the room, 'if you've changed your mind again and want me to look after Jamie, I'm not interested.'

The unexpected tackle pulled Hugo up short. 'I haven't,' he said, and gave her an odd look as he went over to get himself coffee. He stayed by the coffee-table, eyeing her curiously across the small distance between them. 'Whatever put that into your head?'

Without resorting to Anna's heavy-handed insinuations, Paula didn't have much of a reason. 'Nothing. I just thought.' She shrugged and felt a twit.

'Well, whatever you thought, you can set your worried little mind at rest. I told you I'd be making other arrangements.' Hugo smiled sardonically at her discomfort, then suddenly frowned. 'I think it will work out all right. When Jamie starts back at school in September, I'll get someone in full-time.'

'One of your lady-friends, I suppose,' Paula astonished herself with the caustic question.

Hugo's brows shot up above the rim of the cup. He lowered the cup, his mouth curving wryly. 'Lady-friends? How quaint.' The curve broadened into a sly grin. 'You're not fishing about my girlfriends by any chance?'

Paula flared a furious red. 'Don't flatter yourself. I was only concerned about Jamie.'

'I don't get much chance to flatter myself with you around to keep my ego in check, do I?' Hugo laughed teasingly. 'But aren't you the slightest bit curious about my . . . lady-friends . . .?'

'Not the slightest,' Paula lied with a snap as a picture of the very elegant Louise Hunt beamed itself in front of her mind's eye.

'How very unfeminine of you.' Hugo's eyes glistened with amusement. 'However, as it happens, I don't have much time for lady-friends these days, not for one, let alone the hordes I suspect you so generously attribute to me.'

'What about Louise Hunt?' Paula could have bitten off her tongue.

'What about her?' Hugo countered guilelessly, deliberately sidestepping he question.

'She travels with you.' Paula was appalling herself with her curiosity—and amusing Hugo into the bargain.

'So she does,' he agreed blandly, without giving anything away.

And what did she want to know anyway? She could make a pretty good guess at what sort of travelling companion the arrogant brunette was. And it was not her business. Paula was rather surprised Hugo hadn't put her in her place and told her as much.

'You'll probably want to know about Dorothy too,' Hugo offered drily. 'She lives in my apartment.'

That took the wind out of her, and lynx-eyed, Hugo didn't miss her jolt. 'That's made you sit up.' He grinned appreciatively, then said super-casually, 'If it's any interest to you, Dorothy has been with me for about twelve years. She's my housekeeper,' he added.

'It's of no interest to me whatsoever,' Paula shot back indignantly, infuriated that Hugo was playing on her curiosity and knowing she deserved every bit of his amusement.

Hugo raised a sceptical eyebrow. 'I thought not,' he murmured drily, then studied her in silence for a moment or two. 'And when are you going to tell me about yourself?'

Paula gave a start. 'You wouldn't be interested, and there's nothing to tell,' she said shortly. And besides which, you know too much already, she thought, looking away from him. She stood up and took her coffee-cup to the table. 'I'd better get back to the cottage. I need to get on with my work.'

'Is that all you're interested in?' Hugo asked quietly but with an edge in his voice.

'It's important to me,' Paula answered quickly. Too important perhaps, but she had nothing else, and if she messed up the commission this time ... Paula tried not to think about it.

Hugo put his cup down. 'Couldn't you let it go, just for one evening?'

'Why?' she asked abruptly. 'Jamie's in bed.'

Hugo looked puzzled. 'What's that got to do with anything?'

Paula laughed a little harshly. 'It means,' she said pointedly, 'that I've put in my quota of "happy-family" time for one day and you don't need me around any more.'

Hugo's face twisted as if she had hit him. 'I had no idea you felt that way,' he said through thin lips.

Paula flushed. 'I'm sorry, that was rude. I ... I honestly don't mind ... helping you out with Jamie.'

Hugo stared at her. 'Is that what you've been doing?' he asked tonelessly.

'Well, yes. Isn't it?' she countered, dubiously. Did he think she had let him pressure her into staying on for any other reason? Somewhere at the back of her mind a tiny doubt stirred. How much pressure had Hugo really put on her? The answer, uncomfortably, was very little. He had simply told her Roger was coming to the island soon, and taken away her excuse for going back to London—hardly thumbscrew pressure, and she could have left regardless—if she had really wanted to.

Paula met Hugo's eyes uneasily, and had the embarrassing sensation he'd been following her train of thought. She turned away from him. 'I must get back,' she said for the second time, giving Hugo the opportunity to offer to walk her back as he usually did—an act of courtesy, because it was still always light and there was no real reason for him to do it.

'Must you? I was rather hoping you'd come out with me this evening,' Hugo said diffidently.

'Out?' Paula repeated, and then added, 'You mean just you and me—you and I?'

'I can never get the hang of that little point of grammar either.' Hugo smiled, but with an air of covering up nervousness. 'Just to one of the pubs. There's a bit of a gathering on tonight and I thought perhaps you might enjoy it. You've been working so hard on your drawings and I ... we've been taking up a lot of your time. You could do with a break. We both could ... from Jamie ... the house,' Hugo trailed off, shrugging.

Hugo did not need to elaborate; Paula understood what he meant; what she had not realised was he'd been feeling like that too, almost swallowed up by the child's needs and always under that strain of acting as if nothing had happened between them. It hadn't occurred to her Hugo might be finding it as wearing on his nerves as she did.

Paula studied him silently for a moment, noting with surprise the lines of tension around the dark eyes and the faint grey shadow under them. How had she missed seeing that before? Hugo looked as if he needed a break—probably from her, as much as from Jamie.

He would probably go to the pub without her,

and probably have a better time of it too, if she wasn't there to cramp his style. Suddenly, Paula wanted to go with him. 'I'd like to come. Thank you,' she said with a spontaneous smile and saw Hugo's eyes register relief—or so it seemed.

The main room of the pub was bursting at the seams with a few locals and lots of visitors, some unsuccessfully trying to pass themselves off as locals in their too-new heavy homeknits and tweeds. The place was thick with smoke and noisy with talk and laughter. Somewhere from the back came the sound of music—home-made music, not the stereo variety, and above the din of voices talking, other voices were singing in the background. Paula laughed delightedly. Yes, this was what she needed.

Hugo smiled down at her. 'All right?' he asked and she nodded, hanging on to his arm as he edged her through the crush of bodies towards where the music was coming from.

If anything, the back room of the small pub was even more crowded, but with the proportions reversed. A few visitors, and lots of locals—islanders like Anna, with that same ready friendliness and the same blatant, almost child-like curiosity in their faces when Hugo introduced her around. He seemed to know everybody and everybody was delighted to see him.

The thing that struck Paula first was how few young people there were, and how often, when Hugo asked after somebody's son or daughter, he was told that whoever it was was working on the mainland. It was necessity, not the city lights, Paula realised, that took the youth away from the island, and that tourism could not support everybody. The old folk stayed on—or came back, like Sir Iain, when they retired. It made her momentarily sad.

'Ah, you've brought along your lassie,' said a positively ancient man who must have been responsible for some of the music because he had an accordion on his lap. Beside him, a marginally-less ancient one had a mouth organ in one hand, a glass in the other and was bringing each to his mouth in turn.

Paula waited for Hugo to explain that she was not 'his lassie'; Hugo chose not to, but contrarily, as if to confirm everybody's misconception about her role, placed an arm around her shoulder, drawing her closer to himself. It must have been the atmosphere, because it felt natural to have the arm around her as Hugo led her from group to group. Paula's self-consciousness lasted about half a minute and then she didn't give it a moment's thought.

When the singing started again, Hugo astonished her by casually joining in, and fitting into the cheerful unpretentious group in a way that Paula found strangely disconcerting. After a little while she moved away and found herself a chair by the wall from where she could watch and listen—watch mainly, since her eyes stayed fixed on Hugo, drawn by something she couldn't understand.

How many Hugo Camerons were there? Every time Paula turned, there seemed to be a different character facing her, and each a surprise. The real surprise, the part that perplexed her, was that he was prepared to show all the sides of himself so openly. She had seen the arrogant man; was aware of the hard-working businessman; seen the concerned, caring man worried about a small boy; and had glimpsed someone un-expectedly vulnerable that night in the living-room when he had spoken about his brother.

And now, yet another Hugo; relaxed, warm and eminently likeable. It was not just facile charm; he was getting warmth back from his friends in return and you couldn't get that by being charming—or patronising. Like Mark.

Involuntarily, the image rose to her mind. How reserved and up-tight Mark would have been among these islanders whom he would have considered socially inferior. Mark had been a great snob, and the unpalatable part was that some of his attitudes had rubbed off on her; not the snobbishness, she hoped, but that ever-present reserve—always being on guard against showing her real feelings. Paula looked away from the cheerful scene and stared down at her lap, not liking herself very much.

'Embarrassed I'll shatter the glassware?'

Paula glanced up to find Hugo in front of her, smiling teasingly. He sat down beside her. 'Do you like this?' He gestured at everybody and nobody in particular.

'Yes,' Paula said simply.

'Then we must come again.'

She wanted to say, 'yes, let's.' Something stopped her; a shyness. 'I didn't know you were so musical,' she said instead, injecting a softly teasing note into her voice.

A faint smile flickered over Hugo's face. 'There's a lot we don't know about each other, isn't there?' he said, seriously, his voice softly intimate.

That's just what she had realised moments before—and had found so unsettling. Paula tried to laugh off Hugo's seriousness but couldn't think of anything light and amusing enough to counter it. She swung her face away from his gaze, pretending sudden interest in an Anna look-alike who was setting food out on a nearby table. Then Hugo picked up her hand from her lap and drew her to her feet. 'Come on, my girl.' His voice was light and teasing again; the momentarily threatening intimacy gone. 'You're going to have to sing for your supper like everybody else.'

'I can't,' Paula squealed in mock horror.

'Yes, you can.'

Not since before she met Mark had Paula sung songs in a pub—not quite sung, because she didn't know the words to the lilting island melodies. Hugo did that, but she hummed along, laughingly earning her supper, and enjoying herself a lot.

It was the sort of night that would be a blur the next morning. Later, after the supper, when the chairs and tables had been moved aside, Paula caught herself skipping through an unfamiliar reel under Hugo's approving eyes and told herself it was just as well she wasn't going to remember much about 'making an exhibition of herself', she could almost hear Mark saying.

And later still, came the schmaltzy, schmaltzy waltzes. The tenor of the evening changed. Paula watched the oddly-assorted couples on the improvised dance-floor and felt moved. There was something indescribably poignant and romantic about middle-aged and elderly couples gazing into each other's eyes as they danced slowly to the hauntingly sweet music.

'May I?' Hugo asked with a formality that at first Paula took to be ironic and then realised wasn't.

'I ... I'm not dressed for it.' In a fluster of shyness she said the first thing that came into her head.

Hugo flicked his eyes over her skirt and winter cotton shirt, then at the practically identical sensible outfits of the other women. 'If that's the case, then neither is any other woman in the room.' He put an arm around her waist and led her on to the floor.

Paula was conscious of the knowing, approving smiles bestowed on them, and could imagine the innocent gossip running rife tomorrow—about Hugo Cameron and 'his lassie' wrapped in each other's arms on the pint-sized dance-floor in the back room of an old pub. What these nice, friendly people wouldn't know, however, was that by then she and Hugo would have reverted to their careful, impersonal friendliness, with their concern for Jamie providing the only, and very tenuous bond, just like Stephen had between herself and Mark.

Only Paula did not want it to be like that again ... not anymore. She was shocked by the intensity of the resentment she fleetingly felt towards Jamie—and then confused. What was she thinking? That she could be interested in Hugo Cameron if it wasn't for Jamie? That Hugo could possibly be interested in her?

Paula pulled up her thoughts sharply. The evening must have gone to her head. She had known Hugo Cameron for barely two weeks and any interest he had displayed in her was strictly of the standard male variety. And yes, despite his denials, he was still possibly interested in having her be nanny to Jamie for a while. One genuinely pleasant evening together did not change anything, and if she couldn't see that, she was getting soft.

They were very close, their bodies touching and they were dancing so slowly they were swaying to the music rather than dancing. Deliberately, Paula eased herself away from him, and after a moment, felt Hugo's hand withdraw the pressure from her back. Without a word they resumed a 'polite' dancing position, keeping careful distance between them until the music ended. Hugo did not suggest another dance.

In the car, Paula felt on edge and kept up a nervous stream of light remarks to cover it, about the various people they had met that evening, the island in general; and Hugo's remarks were in the same vein—and tone, and came just as readily as hers. If Paula didn't know better, she'd have said Hugo was nervous too.

There was not one gap in the conversation all the way home, but the constant stream of it had the effect of heightening the tension that had sprung up again between them since their last dance, not lessening it. Without even waiting for tomorrow they were back to where they had started from before the evening began—ill at ease with each other under the carefully friendly exterior. And it was best that way, Paula thought with irony, flushing suddenly as she remembered the idiotic thoughts that had drifted in and out of her mind when she had been in Hugo's arms during the first of the dreamy waltzes, before she realised she was being seduced by the music, the warmth of the evening, and by a glimpse of a side of Hugo she found likeable. She needed the drive home to put the evening back into perspective and get a grip on herself.

Then at the cottage door, it all went wrong; Paula turned to him—to invite him in, she supposed for coffee, but she wasn't at all clear about anything because as she looked into Hugo's face, her mind went haywire and everything catapulted out of perspective again.

You can actually ask a man to kiss you without putting it into words; Paula knew her eyes were doing the asking, and in the cold, quite stark light of the moon, Hugo's eyes told her he understood. An anticipatory little shiver shot through her.

'You're cold,' Hugo said, abruptly swinging the door open. He put a hand to her back and gently pushed her inside before Paula took in what was happening—that he'd knocked back her offer. Hugo followed her in, switching on the light as he came in through the door after her.

The harshness of the electric light brought Paula back to her senses. She hid her mortification behind a brilliant smile. 'I've had a lovely evening. Thank you,' she said effusively. They were standing too close, and without the haunting music and the protection of people around them the proximity of Hugo's body was threatening. Paula swung towards the kitchenette. 'Would you like some coffee?' she asked, a proper little hostess all at once and bright as a button in her nervousness.

Hugo reached out and caught her arm before she had reached the safety of the other side of the counter, and in almost a single movement, pulled her back to him and cupped her face roughly with his hands. Paula's lips parted in the hazy second it took for his mouth to reach them.

It was a short, deep, almost angry kiss and her mouth answered on a flare of response before Hugo pulled his mouth away with shattering suddenness, leaving her breathless and confused. Dropping his hands from her face; Hugo stared down at her confusion, then shook his head in a jerky movement and made a sound of frustration. For a split second Paula thought he would kiss her again, and was piercingly aware that she wanted him to.

'I won't stay ... for coffee,' Hugo added with abrupt irony, and Paula felt heat sweep up her face.

And just what else did Hugo think she had been offering? 'As you like,' she returned in a scratchy attempt at off-handedness, mortified she had laid herself open to his assumption that she had been offering anything more than a polite cup of coffee, and a little frightened because far back in her mind something was telling her his assumption was perilously close to the truth.

Hugo turned to the door, then turned back again. 'By the way, I forgot to mention—your publisher is arriving on the ten-thirty plane tomorrow.'

Still floundering in her confusion, Paula was slow to take in his words. 'Roger Harris?' she asked, vaguely, as if she had difficulty coming up with her publisher's name. 'Tomorrow?' Then everything vanished—mortification included, before the rush of the old familiar panic. Roger; the illustrations; they weren't ready; she wasn't ready. 'But why didn't you tell me before?' Paula demanded accusingly.

From the door, Hugo looked at her with sharpened interest. 'It skipped my mind. I'm sorry,' he said. 'I didn't realise it was so important to you.'

'Of course it is. I wouldn't have gone out with you tonight if I'd known,' Paula returned in a wail. It was the way Hugo looked at her, his face tightening after the first flinch, that made her realise how unpleasant, if not downright churlish, that sounded. She hadn't meant it that way. She might be angry and confused, but she couldn't regret the evening—and didn't. She had only meant that she would have felt compelled to stay home and work on her drawings. 'I didn't meant that . . . I . . .' she started again.

'That's all right, you needn't explain. I understood you the first time,' Hugo said tightly.

Paula shook her head in frustration. 'That's just the trouble—you don't understand!' How could he understand how important Roger's assessment was going to be? That her career was virtually on the line? 'Does Anna know?' she asked apropos of nothing, as the domestic arrangements sprang into her mind.

Hugo gave a brief nod. 'Yes. I asked her to prepare one of the guest-rooms.' His eyes drifted slowly across the room towards the silk-screen curtain and stayed there. 'However, if you prefer to put up your boyfriend down here at the cottage, I'm sure Anna won't mind.'

Paula's eyes had followed the direction of his gaze and yet it took a long moment for the innuendo to sink in. Behind the curtain there was one single, very narrow bed. There could be no mistaking Hugo's meaning. Strangely, Paula did not feel angry. She brought her eyes back to Hugo's pinched face and met his eyes, intrigued as to what was going on behind their deep blue façade. Jealousy? Was that what prompted his astonishingly crude innuendo? If it was then it was of the dog-in-the-manger type. Hugo had made it pretty plain he was not particularly interested in her. The male ego was a curious thing, Paula thought, continuing her impassive scrutiny until Hugo dropped his eyes.

'Sorry. I didn't mean that. Forget it,' Hugo muttered, colouring unevenly.

Paula eyed his discomfort with a stab of satisfaction. Not on your life, she thought. She was not going to forget it. And if that was the track Hugo's mind was running along, then she'd make sure that she really gave him something to think about when Roger arrived.

'You'd better ask Neil to drive you to the airport if you want to meet the plane. I'll be busy,' Hugo said curtly.

'Fine,' Paula answered airily—to his back, because Hugo was already out of the door.

She watched him stride with long angry steps up the path. A little way up, he stopped and turned around uncertainly. Paula quickly closed the door. She didn't want him to come back—to apologise or anything else, and in a way was perversely glad the evening had ended on such a sour note. An angry, jealous Hugo Cameron was much less threatening than the warm, likeable man she had been with most of the evening. That one was too attractive by half and she was too vulnerable to him.

Paula glanced at her watch. It was well past midnight but she got out her illustrations, and this time was almost grateful for the seizure of panic that managed to push Hugo Cameron temporarily from her mind.

CHAPTER SIX

As the passengers started to drift out of the plane Paula recognised Sir Iain first and was surprised. Hugo had not mentioned his father's return and she wasn't expecting to see him. Roger was at his heels, grinning cheerfully, large pale eyes blinking with pleasure behind the thick glasses when he spotted her, and, nervous as she was, Paula was glad to see him.

Eyeing her in a way that would have sent her rigid with hostility had it been anyone with better eyesight, Roger kept shaking his head in disbelief. 'I can't believe it.' He turned to Sir Iain. 'I can't believe it's the same woman.'

'Island air,' Sir Iain explained cryptically, imitating his old housekeeper with a wry smile.

Paula chuckled under her breath. Anna's standard explanation for anything she thought wholesome was 'island air'—her euphemism for the gale-force blasts of wind that almost knocked Paula off her feet.

Roger couldn't take his eyes off her. 'You look positively marvellous—just like you used to look before ...' Roger teetered on the brink of the yawning *faux pas*. 'You know ...' He drew back from it with a mumble, faint pink sneaking into the thin, pallid cheeks.

Yes, Paula knew; before the accident, he meant ... and before that even—before Mark drained her personality out of her.

'How have you been getting on with Hugo?' Sir Iain asked chattily on their way to the car, possibly in the misguided belief that he was rescuing the conversation from its sudden dip into the doldrums.

Paula swallowed a mouthful of air and let it out again in a tinny laugh. 'Oh, fine. Jamie is enjoying his uncle's company no end, they're always busy at something. He's been so happy since his uncle's return.' Paula heard herself prattling in a peculiarly high-pitched voice that sounded too jolly for words. 'You'll notice the change. And he can play chess now and . . .' She caught Sir Iain's slightly astonished look and broke off. 'It's nice to have you back, Sir Iain. Did you enjoy your stay in London?' Paula changed the subject hastily and they all talked safely of London during the drive back to the house.

As they pulled up beside Hugo's sleek sports-car at the side of the house, Roger let out a long, low whistle of admiration. 'I say,' he whispered, thrilled, and it was only because Paula could see where his eyes were focused that she realised what the object of his admiration was. Roger in raptures over a car? She'd have credited him with more sense.

Hugo was noticeable by his absence. Anna duly informed them he had taken Jamie sailing for the day and would not be back until later. He was 'very sorry to miss Mr Harris'. She passed on the message in good faith, and Paula for one did not believe it for a moment; but snub or no snub, was quite relieved by his absence. There was an ordeal ahead of her, and after last night's episode she could do without Hugo around to observe her every move—and Roger's.

Lunch was like filling in time before a dentist's appointment. The waiting was always the worst part with that awful sense of inevitability, but Paula would rather have had her teeth yanked out one by one than go through the heart-stopping assessment of her work again.

That was why Roger had come; she knew that. Whatever story he might have tactfully fabricated to get himself an invitation to the island, he had come for one reason and one only: to check on her work. Roger was a businessman, and while most people would have found it difficult to reconcile the nervous, slightly fumbling individual with a very profitable publishing company, Paula knew better. He had given her a second chance after she'd messed up the commission on the first attempt; that had been as a friend. But he had also invested in her work as a businessman, and now had come to check how his investment was coming along. She didn't resent it; she was just terrified.

Roger seemed as nervous as she was when they went down to the cottage after lunch. He picked up the large folder off the table where Paula had left it in readiness for him and took it outside into the brighter light. Paula followed him and watched with detached calm as he settled himself on the bench and placed the folder carefully alongside. Unable to take her eyes off him, she stood by as Roger flicked through the collection—

off-handedly, without poring over them as he had done the first time. He was finished in a matter of minutes, but just sat there staring down at the closed folder. Wondering how to break it to her this time?

There was a bitter taste in her mouth. Paula walked away from him and turned her back. And she had actually thought she had made a good job of them. Her eyelids prickled uncomfortably and she wondered, quite unemotionally, if she was about to cry.

'These will have people stampeding to buy the book. I'll have to rework the print-run, we'll need to do a bigger run first off. Now let me see . . .'

Paula spun around and stared blankly as Roger's brow crinkled into furrows of concentration under the windblown wisps of fair hair. It seemed a very long time before a reluctant hope began to filter through the numbness, like sensation coming back after pins and needles. 'Roger!' she almost screamed. 'Roger, stop rambling and tell me this instant. Are they good?'

Roger came out of his mental maze of figures and peered at her, surprised. 'Of course they're good. They're the best you've ever done.' He frowned, puzzled. 'Couldn't you tell? I thought you were just keeping it back to make me nervous.'

Make him nervous! Paula slumped limply to the ground beside the bench. She wasn't sure whether the muffled sound down in her throat was going to come out a laugh or a cry. 'I don't think I'm ever going to forgive you for this, Roger Harris.'

Roger was truly appalled. 'But honestly, Paula, I didn't mean you to think they weren't good. I thought you knew, really I did.' He was so contrite he looked comic. Paula laughed.

'When can you have the finished artwork ready?' Roger's mind switched back unthinkingly.

'Whenever you like, Roger darling,' Paula laughed again and felt she could do everything overnight on the wild euphoric wave of relief.

Bright-eyed and flushed with pleasure, Roger sprang up and held out a hand. Paula took it and let him draw her to her feet, and they stood facing each other, smiling like two idiots until she took a step towards him and Roger's arms closed around her.

He held her so lightly she could barely feel his arms at first, then very slowly, the hold tightened. Paula put her face against his chest and let out a long, shuddering sigh. Relief and a strange tiredness left her momentarily drained and she could have stayed in the snug cocoon of his arms forever. She stirred reluctantly and lifted her face up from the comforting expanse of new-smelling tweed. 'Thank you . . . for believing in me,' she smiled fondly into his eyes.

'I'm sorry . . . about the way I shocked you last time,' Roger mumbled. 'It was very cruel of me. I . . .'

'It's all right,' Paula intercepted quickly. She didn't want all that brought up again. 'I needed the jolt.'

Roger's eyes wavered over her face and zeroed in closer in slow motion. For a moment Paula was nonplussed by the unfamiliar intensity of his expression, and then, startled, she suddenly realised he was going to kiss her.

Like his embrace, Roger's lips were very uncertain at first, barely brushing her mouth, but when she didn't pull away they seemed to gain confidence and the tentative fluttering turned into a sweet lingering kiss. Unthinkingly, Paula curved her arms around his neck and returned the kiss, but without any of the urgency that Hugo's mouth had drawn from her. Roger's mouth was undemanding. It was an affectionate kiss between two friends. Unthreatening; Paula felt in full control, but when she disengaged herself from his arms Roger seemed embarrassed. He reached jerkily for the folder on the bench.

'I'll take these back to the house with me and study them properly if that's all right with you.' The briskness rang false. 'What are you going to do?'

Paula shrugged lightly. 'I don't know. Laugh . . . sing, cry a little. It hasn't penetrated yet— that the drawings are okay. It'll take time to sink in.' She omitted telling him that her first unaccountable reaction was wanting to rush away and tell Hugo—before she remembered she was angry with him, and that Hugo probably wouldn't be interested anyway.

With the folder tucked under his arm Roger seemed anxious to get away, yet unwilling to go.

'Oh go on, Roger, go and have a good look at them, you're simply dying to. I'll be happy to be alone for a while. I'll see you at the house for dinner this evening.' Paula was all of a sudden anxious for him to go too.

'Ah yes, dinner. That reminds me, what about lunch tomorrow, in town? I'll ask Sir Iain for the car,' Roger suggested, hopefully.

'A celebration? Yes, I'd like that.' Impulsively, Paula planted a kiss on his cheek and gave him a playful shove in the direction of the path. 'Go on now.'

She stood watching him carefully pick his way along the smoother patches of the rough path, looking like a long thin child battling the stiff breeze. When he was out of sight, Paula laughed, a little wildly, savouring the sharp pang of exhilaration, and swept back into the cottage. Laugh; sing; cry a little, she had told Roger. She threw herself on the bed, happy, but too exhausted for anything, and stared at the ceiling, trying to remember how she had felt those other times just after being told her work was great.

It all seemed so long ago, but she could just picture herself rushing to Mark's office to break the news. He hadn't liked her bursting into his office of course, but he must have been pleased for her she supposed, because he had taken her out to dinner. She had drunk a lot, Paula recollected, and they had started bickering. There must have been other occasions with Mark but they can't have been very memorable because her mind was quite blank about them.

The best time had been after her first commission when the impromptu party her friends had put on had gone on until dawn and ended with breakfast in a park. She had been on top of the world—like now, Paula murmured to herself as she fell asleep.

It was very, very quiet when she awakened. Paula lay listening to the stillness. The wind had died down and even straining her ears she could not hear the usual murmur of waves beyond the cottage. Her mind was exquisitely blank. Then the moment passed and recollection flooded back. Roger had liked her illustrations. She could draw again; the spell was broken. Paula stretched luxuriously like a cat, then leapt off the bed.

It was not late and she had plenty of time to take a bath and get ready for dinner without rushing around. She pottered into the tiny kitchen and put the kettle on, then into the even tinier closet of a bathroom to run her bath, all the time her mind toying with the alternatives in her meagre wardrobe.

Paula had two dresses and wore them alternately to dinner at the house when she discovered that Sir Iain maintained a courtly formality and dressed for dinner. Both of them were Mark's preferred style and were almost the same dress, just different colours. Classic wool jersey; high round neck with long sleeves, a fitted bodice over a softly gathered skirt. One was grey, the other navy, and she hated both of them. But she did have something else.

Struck by the sudden thought, Paula raced behind the curtain into the bedroom area and pulled out the suitcase from under the bed. She did bring it, she was sure of it. She rummaged impatiently until her fingers felt the protective plastic wrapping at the bottom of the case.

Very carefully, she drew it out; silk; turquoise. . . . madly Italian—and very Karen Halstead. Her mother had brought the dress home from her last trip to Italy and had tried to badger Paula into wearing it. Around the farm feeding the calves? Paula had protested sourly. There had been nowhere to wear it because she had not gone out since the accident, and besides, she hadn't worn anything so exotic since she'd met Mark. They had been 'too obvious' for Mark's taste.

Karen Halstead had watched Paula pack for this trip, checking her tongue as all the jeans, slacks and sensible skirts went into the case along with the thick warm sweaters, but when it came to the dinner dresses, it had been too much for her and she had taken out the turquoise silk and pleaded in frustration. In the end it had been less trouble to pack it than embark on an all-out argument with her mother. However, the last thing Paula had in mind was actually wearing it.

She gave the dress a light press and laid it on the bed, marvelling at the subtle understatement of the soft, lean lines that were designed to skim the body with just the right amount of sensuousness. Subtle it might be but by contrast the extravagant vee of the neckline was undeniably sexy and Paula found that a little frightening. She wasn't sure that she had the confidence for it any more—if she ever really had in the first place.

After the bath she studied the two sensible alternatives again, then slipped into the turquoise silk and knew exactly how Cinderella must have felt.

The only mirror in the cottage was not full-length and all she could see was vibrant colour around the shoulders and the long slender sleeves, but not much of it in front where the vee dipped down with precarious abandon. The style was not designed to accommodate a bra and there seemed to be an awful lot of creamy expanse left exposed. Paula stared objectively at the valley between the soft curves of breast. Mark would have been shocked. And all at once she was pleased, because she didn't care what Mark would have thought—and would never care again. She felt great, but then had a short sharp moment of doubt when she saw Jamie's face.

The child had come, punctual as always to escort her to the house. When Paula opened the door to him he stood transfixed, staring as if he could not believe his eyes.

'Don't you like it, Jamie?' Paula asked, nervously.

'You look beautiful, Paula,' he said at last in a voice full of awe and as much disbelief, and she was reassured and strangely happy.

Paula gave him a quick kiss as she took his hand. 'Thank you, Jamie.' Her trill of relieved laughter held a rather piercing note of recklessness which the child heard but obviously could not decipher. He looked puzzled.

'And what did you and your uncle do today? Did you go sailing?' Paula sang gaily, and was conscious she came over like a patronising adult.

Jamie nodded, wide-eyed gaze on her flushed face. 'You look different, Paula,' he said doubtfully, still unable to come to grips with the spectacular change in her appearance and manner. And that made two of them.

They walked along in silence for a while, then as they reached the drive, Jamie gave her a sidelong look from under his lashes—an arch sort of look, peculiarly adult, and it sat strangely on the childish features. 'It's for Uncle Hugo, isn't it?' He sprang his observation on her with an almost unpleasant coyness.

And hit the nail on the head.

Paula caught her breath. Angry with the child for his perception; angrier with herself for her transparency, and the fact that while it had lain just beneath the surface of her consciousness, it had taken Jamie's question to make her realise what was really behind her transformation. 'Whatever do you mean, Jamie?' she said stiffly and wondered whether she should race back to the cottage and change.

The boy picked up the hardness in her voice. He flushed guiltily without knowing what it was he had said wrong. 'Nothing, Paula, I didn't mean anything. We had a lovely day out in the boat,' he put in hastily.

Jamie was still prattling carefully about boats, without further mention of 'Uncle Hugo', when they entered the house, and having performed his escort duty, he bolted for it in the direction of the kitchen.

There was a murmur of male voices coming from the living-room. Paula took a deep breath and flung the door open with a defiant flourish. In the silence that followed, the only thing audible was the crackling of the fire.

It was a very long time since Paula had set men on their ears when she walked into a room and she wasn't used to it any more. Horribly self-conscious, Paula took a step into the room, a brilliant smile focused on Sir Iain as the safest target.

'You look charming, my dear.' Sir Iain recovered admirably from his surprise and came forward to greet her.

Roger mumbled something indistinct. Hugo, leaning casually against the fireplace with one hand resting on the mantelpiece, pointedly said nothing but she saw his quick jolt and the odd hard look he gave Roger, and was instantly hostile. Fine, she thought, if that's the way you think it is, but you're not going to spoil my evening—nor Roger's. They had something to celebrate and Paula was determined that celebrate they would.

She didn't need any encouragement when Sir Iain handed her a drink. Downing it in two gulps she was ready for another. All the time the gallant old gentleman kept up a diligent flow of conversation, what about, Paula could not have said, nor had she any idea what was coming out of her own mouth in between the gay little bursts of laughter. By the time Anna came in to announce dinner, Paula had a vague idea the drink in her hand was the fourth.

Anna sucked in her breath in a stage gasp, and after a goggle-eyed start, eyed Paula up and down in the best tradition of a knowing look. From Paula, the gimlet eyes swivelled to Hugo, and then finally to Roger. It was possible the old lady thought her ancient features inscrutable, but even after four drinks in rapid succession, Paula had no trouble reading the awful innuendo in Anna's face. Clearly, the housekeeper thought Paula was rigged up to play *femme fatale*, and if Paula could see it, it must have been positively glaring to everyone else in the room.

'Dinner's ready,' Anna said after she'd done as much staring as her eyes could take in, and nerves shot, Paula gave a silly, high-pitched laugh as if the old lady had made a very funny joke.

If pre-dinner drinks were bad, dinner was worse. Unnervingly aware of Hugo's eyes on her, Paula deliberately concentrated the full beam of her slightly out-of-focus attention on Roger who seemed to go to pieces under the spotlight. He kept running his fingers through his hair, polishing his glasses and blinking inanely around the table. Paula could have shaken him in exasperation; all the more because she had the distinct impression Hugo was silently enjoying her publisher's retreat into helpless awkwardness.

Every time she chanced to glance at him, Hugo's gaze was on her. When he wasn't frozen up in a scowl he was openly—mockingly— admiring; eyes drifting insolently downwards until Paula found herself draping a hand over her bosom like an embarrassed schoolgirl. She knew she was drinking too much; laughing and talking too much. She was just sober enough to know she was quite drunk, and the saner part of her mind hoped desperately she wasn't making too much of an exhibition of herself; the reckless new self that had materialised when she had put on the dress didn't care.

As they were returning to the living-room for coffee, Paula darted upstairs to the bathroom and on her way back encountered Anna at the bottom of the stairs. It was almost as if the old lady had been waiting for her. Paula flashed her a spectacular if remote smile. 'It was a super dinner, Anna; you really excelled yourself tonight,' she gushed airily and was determined to keep the smile in place in the face of Anna's po-faced disapproval.

'Feeling pretty pleased with yourself, are you?' Anna inquired tartly.

Drunk, she meant of course. Paula laughed to hide her embarrassment. The housekeeper was blocking her path and she couldn't get past. Annoyed, Paula could guess what was coming—a lecture on the evils of the demon drink. Anna was a teetotaller, and pretty voluble on the subject once she got started. Paula eyed her in challenge: just try it, she thought belligerently. In her precariously high-voltage mood she was not about to take a sermon—deserved or otherwise—with good grace.

Anna eyed her back. 'I just hope you know what you're doing, my girl.'

Paula frowned. That didn't sound like a preamble to the sermon. 'And what is that supposed to mean?' she returned sharply, but puzzled.

'You know very well what I mean, and it might be all right back where you come from to lead a man on. Yes, that's what I said, lead a man on,' she repeated as Paula's face registered her astonishment. 'It means giving him expectations—false expectations.' Anna's voice gave the words big black underlining. 'It's not nice and it's not kind when your mind is on someone else.'

Paula was stunned. Hugo had expectations? And she was supposed to be interested in Roger? She stared at the old lady in amazement then burst out laughing. If Anna had excelled herself tonight it wasn't just with the dinner. 'You're imagining things, Anna.' Paula shook her head, still laughing softly.

Her face like an angry prune, Anna glared back. 'I've got eyes in my head and there's nothing wrong with them yet, the Lord be praised. The man is in love with you; I know him well enough to read the signs, and if you can't see that then it's not my eyes that need worrying about.'

Paula felt the amusement leave her in waves, washing right out of her. For a moment her heart made strange heavy thumps out of rhythm and crazy thoughts whizzed through her mind. Then she shook her head slowly. Hugo Cameron was not in love with her. He was jealous because he wasn't getting attention and Roger was, and that was simply male ego. Anna had put two and two together and had come up with her standard five. Paula realised she was very angry with the housekeeper for that one brief moment when she had wanted to believe her. 'You've got it all wrong Anna—as usual.' Paula's voice was cold, and shook a little. 'Mr Cameron is no more interested in me than I in him.'

'No?' Anna looked at her strangely, head cocked to one side like an old bird eyeing a curious object. 'But its not Mr Cameron I was talking about, and I know very well what's going on in that direction,' she said, eyes glinting.

Paula flushed. Then Anna said, with a kindish smile, 'It's a two-edged game you've been playing then, lass, without realising it, it seems, and I hope you'll let Mr Harris down lightly.' She turned and padded away down the corridor to the kitchen.

The disbelief came first, then the shock, in that order. Paula stared at the receding scrawny back. Roger? Yes, she had been playing up to him—shamelessly, but that had been to annoy Hugo, not to make Roger think . . . He couldn't possibly be thinking . . .? Paula was appalled. Then she laughed, uneasily. Anna was wrong. It wouldn't be the first time the old lady had jumped to outlandish conclusions, but she had to be sure. Worried, Paula made her way back to the living-room, wishing her head was clearer so she could observe Roger's reactions properly.

She didn't go into the room but stood in the doorway. The three men were standing in different parts of the room, very much as they had been when she had made her first stagy entrance. There was an air of uneasiness between them and Paula wondered vaguely whether it had been present earlier when she had been too self-conscious to notice anything. They all looked at her in something like relief. Ignoring Hugo at the fireplace, Paula smiled at Sir Iain who had started towards her. 'It's been a lovely evening Sir Iain,' she lied brightly. 'Thank you. If you don't mind I won't stay for coffee. I'm rather

tired and would like to get back to the cottage
now.' She looked at Roger, still under the
portrait of some fierce-looking Cameron in a kilt.
'Will you walk me back please, Roger?' she asked,
casually, she hoped. She was suddenly nervous of
him but had to get some time alone with him to
reassure herself that Anna had been wrong,
otherwise she would never sleep.

Hugo was at her side, with a hand at her elbow
while Roger was still looking about for somewhere
to put down his glass of port. 'I'll see you back,'
Hugo muttered without looking at her and bundled
her into the hall before Paula could object.

'I asked Roger to take me back,' Paula snapped
as they left the house. The cold was biting after
the warmth of the house and she gave a sudden
shiver, wishing she'd thought to bring a jacket
with her. Hugo peeled off his jacket. 'No, don't.
I'm all right.' She tried to forestall him,
churlishly. He ignored her protest and put the
jacket around her shoulders, then wrapped his
arm around for good measure. Paula let both of
them stay there; she needed the warmth from the
one and the support from the other because her
feet were unused to high heels at the best of
times, and this was far from being one of them
when the drink seemed to have moved from her
head to her feet, and she practically required
propping up just to stand. 'I said I asked Roger,'
she started again in a belligerent mutter.

'I'm not deaf. I heard you,' Hugo interrupted
testily. 'And if you weren't so drunk you'd
remember that we haven't got a seeing-eye dog
on the estate to bring him back to the house

again. What did you have in mind, walking each other up and down the path all night?' he asked sourly.

She hadn't thought of Roger's poor eyesight. Paula had a sudden vision of herself and Roger, the half-blind leading the half-drunk, and vice versa. It was funny, momentarily, and she sniggered in spite of herself, then was annoyed that Hugo had to make his point so cuttingly. 'It was very kind of you to be so considerate of Roger,' she said snakily.

'Not at all,' he contradicted with sarcastic politeness. 'Your precious Roger can break his neck for all I care, only it'd be damn inconvenient having him do it here.'

There wasn't much to say to something so nasty, but furious at his callousness, Paula gave a sideways twist in an attempt to get herself out from under his arm. She stumbled.

'What are you trying to do now, break your neck?' Hugo's fingers sank savagely through the jacket into the soft flesh of her upper arm.

'You'd like that wouldn't you?' she taunted, sounding appallingly childish—or plain drunk. 'Or would that be inconvenient too?'

'Don't be absurd.' Hugo pushed her in through the cottage door and went straight into the little kitchen.

'Just what do you think you're doing?' Paula demanded, standing at the counter that separated the cooking-area from the living-room.

'Making you coffee,' Hugo replied, his back to her as he filled the kettle. 'You could do with a gallon—or two.'

'Am I supposed to construe from that that you think I'm raving drunk?' Paula asked tartly.

Hugo threw a glance over his shoulder. 'Thinking doesn't come into it. Why don't you sit down before you fall down,' he suggested curtly.

Paula hesitated then moved to the table. She tossed his jacket over the back of a chair and sat down. Her feet were killing her; she eased them out of the pinching grip of the shoes and would have liked to have done something similar for the tightness around her head. Looking up, she caught Hugo studying her from the kitchenette.

CHAPTER SEVEN

'SHEDDING the glad rags already?' Hugo inquired mockingly. 'Pity, I rather like you like that.' His eyes fixed on the flesh between the vee of the front. Paula's hand twitched but she resisted the urge to bring it up over her breast as she had been doing half the night.

'You should doll yourself up more often,' Hugo observed with a mirthless smile. 'It's quite a change from the ubiquitous jeans and sensible skirts which is all I ever seem to see you in—not forgetting that bunny-rug of a dressing-gown of course.'

Paula contemplated him with dislike. 'You just can't help yourself, can you? Sneer, sneer, sneer. You have to spoil everything,' she said with a weary contempt. 'You do it deliberately. You did it deliberately tonight—turned the evening into a fiasco with your sneering and that air of superior amusement. Don't think I didn't notice.'

The flush darkening his face told her the contempt had found its mark. 'Frankly, I'm amazed you noticed anything,' Hugo returned angrily.

'I'm not that drunk. I may have had a few too many but there's no need to imply I'm ready for Alcoholics Anonymous. Damn it, I was happy this evening—really happy. Roger was happy too, and you had to go and spoil everything for us.'

Paula raged at him like a thwarted child. At the back of her mind she knew she was being unreasonable to lay the blame for the wretched evening at Hugo's feet. It had been her fault as much as his. But if he hadn't insinuated there was something between herself and Roger in the first place, it wouldn't have occurred to her to act as if there was.

'The drink's gone to your imagination. I did not spoil anything,' Hugo said huffishly. 'And what was I supposed to be doing anyway— flinging bouquets and congratulations all around the place?'

So Roger had mentioned the illustrations after all, Paula thought, surprised; he must have done for Hugo to know about them. Hugo hadn't said a word; that was to be expected, but Paula was a little hurt that Sir Iain had not commented. 'It wouldn't have killed you to be a little bit pleasant. Today meant a lot to me—and to Roger. We had a lot to celebrate.'

Some of the colour went out of Hugo's face. 'Did you now?' The voice suddenly turned ugly.

Paula eyed him sullenly. Hugo could have no idea of what she had been through; no idea of the self-doubt—nor of the mind-blowing relief which he just put down to drunkenness. He didn't know how supportive Roger had been, nor how much she owed him. 'Yes, we did,' she muttered angrily.

Hugo said in the same ugly, very controlled voice, 'Then you should have made an announcement at dinner and let us all join in the happy occasion.'

Stand up beating her chest and announce her

illustrations were the greatest? For all the inhibition-loosening drink, Paula had been too shy to refer to them. She had expected Roger to say something though, propose a toast, or whatever, to their success. She was disappointed that he hadn't. 'It was up to Roger,' Paula said, her voice faintly reproachful.

'Hmm. Not much of a one for initiative, is he?' Hugo jeered. 'But then he probably exhausted his supply of it this afternoon.'

'What are you talking about?' Paula's voice sharpened with suspicion while her fuzzy brain tried to work out the obscure insult to Roger.

Hugo showed his teeth. 'I'm talking about your heart-warming little scene outside the cottage this afternoon, very touching. Was that before or after he popped the question?'

Paula nearly fell off the chair.

'Don't worry,' Hugo assured her smoothly, his eyes hard. 'I didn't stay around to observe. I don't get my kicks that way. I was coming down to apologise for being so churlish last night. You happened to be in a clinch with your publisher— fiancé, I assume he is now, and while I know you don't credit me with any sensitivity, I left without intruding on the tender moment.'

Paula wasn't listening. She stared, wide-eyed and then became conscious that her mouth was open. She snapped it shut. So that's what Hugo had been getting at; he thought she and Roger had become engaged that afternoon, and that's why she had dressed herself up and carried on a treat. Hugo's face was tight, the bones of his jaw standing out in sharp, hard lines.

The kettle started its ear-splitting whistle and Hugo swung around to it. Paula stared at his back, noticing, almost mechanically, how rigid the shoulders were under the white shirt. Hugo was seized up—literally, with jealousy. She must have made a better job of her performance than she realised. Suddenly Paula wanted to laugh, but the next moment it wasn't funny at all. If that was Hugo's interpretation of her behaviour—on top of Anna's insinuations—then what about Roger? What was he thinking? Paula didn't want to know. She felt dreadful.

Hugo brought the cup of coffee to the table and slammed it down in front of her with just enough restraint not to break the cup. Paula looked down at the cup. 'I'd like you to go now, please,' she said miserably.

Hugo either didn't hear her or simply ignored her. 'And is this engagement going to drag on for fourteen months too?' he asked softly, and Paula was shocked again—angry-shocked this time. She jerked her head up. Hugo's eyes took stock of her shock with blatant satisfaction. 'I gather long engagements are rather in your line,' he said, chattily.

He knew about Mark; she had already worked that out, but until this moment, hadn't realised just how much. 'Your father had no right to . . .'

'My father has nothing to do with anything. Leave him out of this,' Hugo cut her off sharply.

'He's told you about Mark.'

'Not much—I had to find most of it out for myself.'

'How?' Paula demanded, when she really meant 'why'.

'By asking around,' Hugo replied casually. 'I've a lot of contacts, it wasn't difficult,' he smiled, self-deprecatingly, as if he didn't want to boast.

She knocked over the cup as she sprang to her feet and didn't even notice. Some of the hot coffee splashed on to the dress; Paula did not notice that either. 'How dare you go snooping and prying into my private business.' She was shaking with rage, wanting to lash out—wanting mostly just to hit him.

Hugo stood his ground, but tensed up as if on guard against a palm possibly flying at his face. 'I wanted to know about you, more than my father was prepared to tell me,' he said evenly. 'And I had no other way of finding out because you've been so determined not to let me through that nine-foot barrier you've built around yourself.' His mouth twisted. 'I slipped up about Harris, though, didn't I? How long has that little affair been going on?'

'You had no right,' Paula spluttered, choking with fury.

'That's neither here nor there,' Hugo dismissed his invasion of her privacy with infuriating nonchalance. 'But since you bring it up, I consider I have every right to an explanation.'

'Explanation? For what?'

'How about for leading me on, for a start, letting me think you were interested,' Hugo suggested nastily.

Old Anna's accusation almost word for word,

only it was Roger she was supposed to have been leading on. And now Hugo? Paula grated out an involuntary laugh at the absurd irony of it and threw back the same answer she had thrown at Anna. 'You're imagining things.'

'Am I? Then what was that night all about—when I got back from London? And what about last night? If that wasn't an invitation, I don't know what is, so don't try to tell me I'm imagining things and that you're not interested. You practically exploded in my arms, Paula, but if I'd tried to take you up on it, you would have backed off just like the other night when your frigid little self took over.' Hugo was so angry there was a tremor running through his body, but he taunted her with deliberate coolness, probably guessing that it would infuriate her more than hot anger.

'Typical!' Paula screeched. 'The standard male jibe! You couldn't get me into bed, so now I'm supposed to be frigid.'

'Couldn't?' Hugo pulled back and studied her sarcastically. 'Couldn't?' He shook his head, his lips twisting with malice. 'You know perfectly well I could have—and that you wanted me to; but you wanted me to seduce you into it so that you wouldn't have to take responsibility for your own feelings. You wanted me, Paula—still want me but can't admit it. I doubt you've admitted your real feelings in your life—to yourself, let alone anyone else. They frighten you silly, don't they? Which is why you need to get yourself engaged to prigs like Mark Naughton and helpless fumblers like Harris. You can handle them. They're unthreatening because they don't ask for much and will always be satisfied with the little you choose to give of yourself.'

Every word hit a nerve but the anger saved her. 'That's because they're not egomaniacs who think they're God's gift to women,' she hissed back. 'Roger Harris is worth dozens of you. And if you'd done your snooping a bit better you'd know he's been my friend and publisher for years. He's a good man. A kind, considerate, decent man.' Paula crowded in every adjective and would have put in more only she ran out of them.

Hugo laughed in her face. 'I don't doubt he's all those wonderful things, but if you've been playing the same game with him as you have with me, then he must also be a very frustrated man.'

Another moment and she would launch herself at him in frenzied mindless attack. 'Don't judge every man by your own low-down standards. If you were more like him you wouldn't be assuming that just because a woman happens to kiss you she wants to fall into bed with you!'

'Doesn't she?' Hugo smiled unpleasantly. 'That wasn't the message I got,' he said with soft menace and a fixed glittering look in his eyes that set warning bells clanging in her head—too late.

Paula shook her head wildly and raised a hand to ward him off, pushing against his chest. Hugo made a sound of angry derision as he snapped his fingers over her wrist and swung it down unceremoniously, wrenching it behind her and in the same moment plunged his other hand into the curls at the back of her neck using the vicious grip to force her head back. The pain momentarily blocked out the panic. Paula mouthed a soundless cry before his mouth blocked that out too.

There were no preliminaries. Hugo was not out to cajole with teasing or tenderness. He was hurting her and didn't care. With her free hand Paula made frantic attempts to push him away then gave up and stopped the ineffectual struggling altogether. But passivity was not what Hugo wanted. His mouth rammed violently, demanding response, and was not going to stop until it got what it wanted and she was just as determined not to give in to it.

Hugo released her wrist and eased himself away from her a little. Paula felt his hand insinuating itself into the silk front of the dress and with a gentleness that was at variance with the fiercely probing mouth, close over her bare breast. For a moment it lay still over the soft roundness, then the expert fingers began to do tormentingly exciting things to the hardening nipple. Paula's reaction was sudden and shattering. She arched uncontrollably under his hand and with a blinding explosion of urgency abandoned herself to sheer mindless sensation.

That was what Hugo had wanted. He gave a low, satisfied growl deep in his throat as her body took over, answering his demands with demands of its own, and when nothing mattered except easing the unbearable hunger, Hugo pulled back, eyes glowing darkly with his victory, and with something in their depths that looked quite crazy. 'Now tell me you don't want me,' he breathed at her.

Paula could not tell him anything because she had to fight to get enough air back into her lungs just to breathe. She shook her head dumbly. Hugo's lips curved tauntingly as he cupped his hands around her face and tilted it back. The lips were very gentle this time, and menacingly tender as his body moved against her with a controlled sensuousness, intent on rousing away her last shred of self-possession.

With a vague, cloudy awareness, Paula knew what he was doing to her: manipulating her body, using every trick in the book from violent passion to unbearable gentleness. And her body was revelling in every touch, crying out for more. It was no use denying it: she wanted Hugo Cameron as she had never wanted any man before.

Drawing back suddenly Hugo studied her flushed face through half-closed lids, examining it pore by pore. 'And do you think Roger Harris is going to make you feel this way?' he jeered softly.

She hit him then—across the face, with an unthinking, stinging swipe.

It took Hugo a fraction of a second to react and then he grabbed both her arms and twisted them savagely behind her back. 'You little she-devil,' he hissed as the ugly stain of colour surged into his cheek where her palm had landed. Then unexpectedly Hugo made a harsh grating sound that was a laugh of sorts, but his eyes stayed savage. 'I'm flattered, since that's more reaction than poor Harris is ever going to get out of you.' His face was very close. Paula could feel his hot breath brushing her cheek as she tried to avert her face. 'This is the real you, Paula, the one you've been trying to hide from yourself for so long, the passionate, demanding one that you're so scared of.' Hugo released her abruptly.

The chair was behind her. Paula could feel the edge of it at the back of her knees. She lowered herself on to it before her shaky legs gave out. Hugo took a step closer and she lifted a hand protectively in front of her, looking at him dumbfounded.

Hugo bent down to her, his face contorted with emotion that wasn't anger any more, and Paula dropped her eyes, fixing them unseeingly on his feet. Unable to move, she listened with a cold motionless tension as his words rained down on her head in an urgent impassioned torrent. 'You can't marry Roger Harris, Paula. He's wrong for you, you must see that. Yes, you'd be able to call all the shots—the guy worships the ground you walk on, anyone can see that. Only you don't want a man like that Paula, any more than you wanted Mark Naughton. You want . . .'

Paula flipped her head up like a puppet. 'A man like you?' she jeered, her voice small and scratchy but vibrating with the anger that was coming back to life. Hugo shrugged with an easy arrogance that sent a bolt of trembling fury through her. 'I wouldn't marry you, Hugo Cameron, if you were the last man on earth.' Not very original but she was surprised she could come out with anything at all. The words bounced off him without rippling a line of his expression.

'Then it's just as well for me that I haven't asked you, isn't it?' Hugo smiled derisively as he looked down at her but his eyes wanted to kill her. Some of her scorn had penetrated his pride. Paula registered the look and stored it away mentally. Later, she might derive some kind of compensatory satisfaction that she had managed to prick his ego just that tiny bit.

She stared up, hating him. 'If you've quite finished psychoanalysing me, I suggest you get out.' She rose to her feet with a painful show of dignity, pushed past him and strode to the door. Paula flung it wide open, keeping her hand on the knob. 'I want you out. Now.' The scene was straight out of a melodrama but with some of the effect of her stance diminished by her stiockinged feet and the large brown stain down the front of the dress.

Hugo picked up his jacket and came across the room unhurriedly. Every muscle in Paula's face felt like granite in the effort to prevent herself from dissolving into a heap in front of him.

'Congratulations—on your latest engagement.' Hugo got in the last soft parting shot before she could slam the door on him.

Eyes clamped shut, Paula leant against the closed door waiting for the impact of the shock to pass before she could trust herself to make it to the bed. Her mind was numb and she felt as if Hugo had peeled away layer upon layer of skin to expose something very vulnerable within her.

He was wrong about Roger; she could have told him there wasn't any engagement, nor would there be. It might have stopped him but Paula doubted it. Roger had not really been the issue tonight, only the springboard from which Hugo had launched his attack, as if he had only been waiting for an opportunity to break through the barrier he accused her of having built around herself.

And he was right there; something had happened to her during her relationship with Mark, a closing-in process, while after Mark she had become more closed in than ever. But how had Hugo known, guessed what lay behind the barrier? How could he possibly have suspected she was afraid of opening up to her feelings, needs? Frigid, he had called her and meant to hurt. Was she? Her shattering responses to him made Paula question that. The word wasn't frigid, it was distrust; she was riddled with it— distrust of herself, her own motives, and where before it had been of Mark's motives, now it was Hugo's.

What did Hugo want from her? Really want? As he pointed out so crudely, he could have bedded her without any trouble—and hadn't, so he couldn't be simply after a bedmate for his stay on the island. A nanny for Jamie? He denied that, but then Mark would have denied that he'd wanted her just as a stepmother for Stephen. What people—men, said and what they really wanted were two totally different things.

Paula opened her eyes and took in the messy table with the coffee-cup still precariously perched on its side right at the edge of the table. She looked down blankly at the ruined dress, then very slowly, as if it was an effort just to put one foot in front of the other, made her way to the bedroom area. Ripping off the soft silk, Paula hurled it into the corner where it fell in a bedraggled little heap.

Without bothering to undress further, she climbed into bed and hugged herself tightly around the shoulders, knees drawn up into her stomach as if she had the most terrible pain there. She rocked herself to and fro, moaning softly. The pain wasn't in her stomach and it wasn't anything that could be put to rights by an aspirin. 'I'm going to leave,' was her last conscious thought.

In the morning Paula woke with the vague feeling that she had to get away from something, and then she remembered: the something was Hugo and she was going to leave. Not today; she had no energy for that, but tomorrow she would get herself on to the first plane off the island.

Paula stretched out her right leg and jiggled it under the blanket. It felt fine and she had no recollection of a nightmare. Small mercies. Her head seemed all right, too—no hangover, just a terrible burnt-out feeling inside her brain that had nothing to do with the drink she had consumed. It made it very hard to think straight and she supposed she ought to be grateful for that.

She was bathed and dressed and toying with the idea of a long, hard walk along the beach when Roger turned up. She had already reasoned out that last night had nothing to do with him; that he'd probably have a mild stroke if he knew he was supposed to be engaged to her, but with

all the innuendoes that had been hurled about by
Hugo and Anna, Paula was instantly nervous at
the sight of him.

'Have you forgotten our lunch?' Roger peered
worriedly into her face.

Oh God. Lunch—alone with Roger. 'No. No,
of course not,' Paula lied through her teeth with a
bright smile. Her mind raced over the range of
excuses to get out of the date and couldn't come
up with any. 'I've been looking forward to it,' she
lied again out of sheer guilt.

'Good. That's good,' said Roger, grinning in
relief. He looked her up and down. 'If you're
ready we can make a start now, can't we? It's
going on for twelve-thirty.'

Paula was wearing the 'ubiquitous jeans' with a
warm pullover, no make-up and was aware she
must look as if she'd just got up off her death-
bed. 'Yes, I'm ready,' she replied carelessly, then
experienced a twinge of guilt because it was so
obvious she had not gone to any trouble for their
celebratory lunch.

There was no sign of Sir Iain's elderly sedan
when they reached the house; only Hugo's
shining extravaganza was poking its long sleek
nose out of the garage by the side of the house.

Roger walked right up to the garage and stuck
his head in, came out and looked around
uncertainly. 'It's not here. I can't understand it.
I asked Sir Iain yesterday about using the car
today.'

A mean little hope flared up. 'Neil may have
taken it somewhere. We might have to leave it for
today.' Paula caught sight of Hugo strolling out of

the front door of the house. 'Let's go back to the cottage,' she begged, momentarily reduced to panic at the prospect of an encounter. Her face froze as Hugo sauntered towards them, hands in pockets and looking none the worse for the late night.

He nodded curtly and Paula stared through him. 'You look as if you've lost something.' Hugo addressed Roger with a dryness just this side of a sneer.

Roger flushed. 'No ... that is, do you know where the car has gone? Your father's car.'

'Yes,' Hugo said shortly. 'Neil's taken Anna into town for the shopping—and Jamie as well. Why? Was he to have waited for you?'

Roger frowned. 'Into town? But I thought the car would be free today. Sir Iain didn't say anything about a shopping expedition. I should have checked I suppose,' he trailed off, embarrassed.

'It doesn't matter,' Paula said hastily, placing a hand on his arm wanting to lead him away as quickly as possible. Hugo was studying Roger with a snide amusement that made her hackles rise. He had been insulting enough about Roger last night and she was not going to let Roger stand around now and be sneered at.

'Were you planning on going somewhere?' Hugo asked Roger with some interest.

Roger gave a distracted grin. 'We had planned lunch in town.' His eyes had wandered longingly towards the expanse of glistening dark blue metal sticking out from the side of the house. Hugo followed his gaze and his shoulders gave a noticeable jerk of surprise.

Paula nearly yelped with shock. She stared at Roger, horrified. He couldn't possibly be thinking . . . ? 'It's all right, Roger, let's just leave it. We can go another day.'

There was a long silence and nobody moved. They all studied the exotic vehicle as if none of them had ever seen it before, then Roger turned to Hugo. 'I wonder, Hugo, whether you'd trust me with your car, if you're not planning to use it yourself, that is.'

Hugo's face was expressionless. Paula stared at him. 'Don't let him,' she beamed the message with her eyes.

'I'm not really sure,' Hugo began dubiously. 'It's not the easiest car to handle if you're not familiar with it.'

It was the worst thing he could have said.

'I'd have thought it'd be just like any other car,' Roger muttered, piqued at Hugo's implication that his driving skills were not up to handling it. He recovered himself almost immediately. 'That's all right, Hugo, silly of me to ask. I can see it's a very expensive machine.'

The snipe was intentional, and, coming from Roger, unexpected. A harsh, dark red seared up Hugo's throat. His eyes flashed with dislike. 'You're most welcome to borrow it, of course,' he said stiffly and Paula could have kicked him— kicked both of them for being so childish.

Hugo avoided her eyes. 'I'd better explain a few things to you,' he said to Roger.

Roger threw her a blissful glance over his shoulder and sprang after Hugo at a gallop—an excited little boy dying to try out a new toy—

somebody else's toy at that.

She would refuse to go. It was not that Paula particularly distrusted Roger's driving; he was a competent driver and his less than average eyesight made him an especially careful one. But in a car he had never driven before? Along the island's narrow, winding roads? Her nerves were not up to that sort of challenge, not this morning. Paula marched up to the car, ready to tell him so.

Roger was in the driver's seat with Hugo leaning in explaining the intricacies of his toy to him. Paula stood by, seething with annoyance. Hugo finally finished his lecture on the knobs and dials on the dashboard, and straightening up, looked her hostile face over carefully. 'You're looking rather pale, Paula,' he said casually in what must have been the understatement of the year. 'Perhaps you'd prefer to leave the outing for another day. Roger and I can go for a run in the car.'

Hugo was giving her the opportunity to plead headache—or something; making it easy for her, and she should have felt grateful and snatched up the cue instead of bristling with resentment. There was anxiety in Hugo's eyes—doubtless for his precious machine in Roger's inexperienced hands, and that was the last straw. 'Thank you for letting us borrow your car Hugo,' Paula said with stony politeness and started moving towards the passenger side.

'Don't be an idiot,' Hugo hissed, gripping her arm and preventing her from getting into the car. He flicked a glance into the car where Roger sat examining the dashboard with a concentration that momentarily excluded everything, and everybody. 'I want to talk to you,' Hugo said urgently.

Paula tried to pick his fingers off her arm. 'You had your say last night,' she returned in an angry hiss. 'Wasn't that enough for you?'

Hugo winced. 'For God's sake, Paula, I didn't mean all those things I said last night. I had no right to talk to you like that. I'm sorry, believe me.'

Paula looked him fully in the face. 'You meant them,' she said coldly, and as Hugo dropped his hand, got into the car slamming the door behind her with a viciousness that made the car shake.

Roger set the car into motion with a jump out of the garage that had Hugo springing sideways for safety. Let him worry, Paula thought meanly, catching the final look of consternation on Hugo's face. They lurched for a bit but Roger seemed to be getting the hang of it as they followed the winding track through Sir Iain's estate. At the end of it, where it joined the main road, Roger stopped. 'What would you say if, instead of going into town, we drove to the little village on the Butt and had lunch at the pub there?'

Paula smiled tightly. The Butt was miles away across the island and would take ages to reach, especially if they went via the winding coastal road. She could see right through the ingenuous suggestion; the longer the drive, the more time in his borrowed plaything. Strange she had missed the streak of childishness in Roger. Paula shrugged. 'It's up to you, Roger,' and the token assent was all he needed. Roger swung the car left instead of right, happy as the proverbial sandboy, and Paula leaned back in her seat in sulky silence.

They went the coastal road—of course. It took forever and by the time the village finally came into sight at the bottom of the steep slope that ran towards the sea, Paula was tired, headachey and surprisingly hungry. Added to which, she was still very much annoyed with Roger for his unexpected display of childishness.

Roger parked the car outside the tiny pub and gave her a sheepish grin as he helped her out. 'I'm rather keen on cars, my secret passion.'

'I'd never have guessed,' Paula returned snappishly.

Roger coloured. 'You must think I'm an awful idiot. I know Hugo did, but it's not every day I get the chance to drive the car of my dreams,' he explained leading her into the tiny pub.

Paula had already learnt that time was not a precious commodity on the island; everyone had plenty of it and the proprietor's wife might never have heard of clocks. If someone wanted lunch at three o'clock in the afternoon that was fine by her, and when the accommodating lady eventually emerged from the kitchen, Paula was so hungry she could have eaten the leg of the chair instead of the rack of lamb presented to them with a self-conscious flourish.

By the end of the meal, hunger appeased, irritation washed away by several glasses of excellent claret, Paula felt a new woman and Roger was quick to sense the adjustment of her mood in his favour. 'I hope you've forgiven me for my childishness?' he asked, still a little diffident.

Paula laughed. 'Was I so obvious? I didn't mean to be so bad-tempered about it. It was a beautiful lunch, Roger. Thank you. I suppose we ought to make a start back,' she added, without enthusiasm, too relaxed and mellowed to want to move.

Roger examined his wrist. 'After four, but we've time for a walk down to the cove before heading back, if you'd like to, that is. I know a nice spot down there,' he suggested with a peculiar earnestness, and Paula felt her earlier nervousness stirring back to life.

'That sounds nice,' she agreed tentatively, on guard, but obliged to put herself out to make up for her previous display of bad temper.

CHAPTER EIGHT

THEY had not thought to bring a rug but some thoughtful person had long ago erected a seat of sorts out of smooth rounded stones, and they sat on that, watching the sea lapping into the delicately tinted sands of the small bay. The silence felt awkward already, or was that her imagination working overtime? Roger put an arm around her shoulder. 'There's something I wanted to talk to you about,' he started and Paula seized up inside. She shifted her position a little, intending to stand up, walk about, anything to put off what she was afraid was coming.

Roger's arm tightened around her. 'Don't get up yet.'

Paula looked at him uneasily and even prepared as she was, gave an involuntary start at the expression on his face; Roger had looked just like that a moment before he had kissed her the day before, that same unfamiliar intensity.

Paula swerved her face away and suddenly bent down to pick up a stone lying at her feet. She had to stop his next words, whatever they were, before he hurt himself by voicing them. She was too slow. As she straightened up, Roger said, 'I love you Paula. You must know that. I've loved you for years, ever since we met.' The words tumbled out in a desperate stream as if he couldn't get them out quickly enough. 'I meant to tell you then, only I'm such a slow-witted fool and Mark got in first. It was hell for me, then after the accident, I thought there might be hope for me again, only I couldn't bring myself to speak to you about it because you seemed all shut in on yourself, taking Mark's death so hard, and Stephen's. It's only now that you seem, well, more like you used to be—alive and glowing. And yesterday when I held you in my arms, I wanted to ask you then. Oh hell, Paula, I'm trying to ask you to marry me and I'm making my usual hash of it.'

Hugo had been right—half right anyway. That was Paula's first uncontrollable thought. Hugo had spotted Roger's intention with deadly accuracy, only he'd been a day premature. She had wanted to laugh then, but the joke was on her. Except that it wasn't a joke and the laugh now welling up dangerously inside her was hysteria; she would die of mortification if it came out, and so would Roger.

Paula could not look at him while she tried to get a grip on her crazy reaction. She fumbled around in her dazed mind for words that would sound less hurtful than a blunt 'no'. 'Roger dear,' she began gently, forcing herself to meet the expectant eyes that were fixed on her unblinkingly. 'Please don't think that I don't care for you, I do, very much. I'm very fond of you,' she struggled on. How to go on without that soul-destroying 'but'? 'It's just that . . .' Paula shook her head dumbly and saw the light flicker out behind the thick lenses.

'Then it was only happy relief yesterday?'

Roger's lips twisted with faint bitterness. 'I should have realised. I should have realised it didn't mean anything to you.' He continued to stare at her, frowning at first, then nodding slowly, as if something was becoming clear to him. 'Of course,' he murmured softly under his breath. 'I'm too late again, aren't I?'

Paula looked back at him perplexed.

Roger gave a small, tight smile. 'Hugo Cameron,' he muttered, 'of course.'

The denial sprang to her lips but stayed unvoiced. Let him think that, Paula thought. Let him think she was interested in someone else if it made him feel any better, less hurt. It didn't matter whether he picked on Hugo or anybody else.

'I should have tried harder earlier,' Roger said, without rancour. 'There might have been hope for me then, even while Mark was alive.' He looked at he oddly and said suddenly. 'You never meant to marry Mark, did you?'

The unexpectedness, not to say accuracy of the question caught Paula off-balance. 'I . . . I don't know,' she said evasively.

Roger nodded, peculiarly satisfied. 'Mark always felt you wouldn't,' he said astonishingly and Paula felt her blood run cold.

'What?'

Roger flushed slightly. 'I shouldn't be talking to you like this, it's not my business. It's just that I gathered from something Mark said quite a long time before the accident, that he had the feeling you wouldn't go through with the marriage. I should have made my move then.' Roger's mind switched back to his own train of thought, his own regrets. He had no inkling of the implication of what he had just told her.

How could he? He didn't know she had been blaming herself for the accident, thinking it was the shock of her statement that had made Mark momentarily careless at the wheel. But if Mark had suspected all along that she wouldn't marry him, then he can't have been surprised when she came out with it. He certainly could not have been shocked. Paula's emotions came back to life. She turned on Roger, breathless, angry. 'Why didn't you tell me before? Why did you keep it back from me?'

Roger looked nonplussed. 'What? Keep what back?'

Paula shook her head in frustration. It was pointless railing at him for his silence, pointless to tell him he had unwittingly let her carry the awful guilt for a year. 'Let's go back now,' Paula said, feeling as if she had been kicked in the stomach. Was that relief? She had never felt more ill.

'Yes, very well.' Roger wasn't sure what to make of the change in her. 'It looks like rain,' he observed dismally.

About three miles out of the village the first drops fell. Large and heavy. Roger made an agitated attack on the knobs and dials in front of him and by the process of elimination, finally managed to hit the right one and sent the windscreen wipers swishing across the wide expanse of glass. In those few moments the rain had thickened into a dark mass and the wipers seemed to make very little difference to the visibility.

Paula gripped the edge of the seat tightly as they ploughed in lurches through the wall of water. She tried to quell the rising panic but as Roger missed the curve in the track and the car gave a sudden lunge to the left, a tiny scream jolted itself out of her before she could stop it. 'I'm sorry,' she mumbled.

Roger switched off the engine.

'I'm sorry,' Paula said again. 'I just got a little fright. We don't have to stop. I'm okay, really,' she tried to assure him.

'You might be, I'm not. I can't see, damn it,' Roger said through his teeth. 'I can't risk going on.'

'But if we go very slowly?'

Roger shook his head. 'Too dangerous. I don't know the road well enough to drive by instinct, and the wretched car has a mind of its own. Not my day, is it?' He smiled weakly and looked as if he wanted to howl—and just might.

Paula reached out a hand and gave him a small pat on the arm. 'It's not the end of the world, Roger.'

'No, but jolly inconvenient. We'll have to sit here and hope the rain eases enough for me to try and go on—or at least get us back to the village. And pray that that's before dark.' He gave an angry laugh. 'Because I wouldn't trust myself to handle this chariot in the dark, either. Can't win, can I?'

An hour later when they were still sitting there in dispirited silence, Paula forced herself to face a few unpleasant facts: the rain was not going to stop; Roger had given up on the day and was resigned to sitting it out for as long as it took, and that looked like being all night; no one was going to come by and rescue them. The next move was up to her.

'I'm going to walk back to the village,' Paula said with sudden decision. 'Don't look so horrified, it's only a few miles.' She glossed over that bit lightly. 'When I get there I'll find a couple of men to drive me back here, then one of them can drive this car back to the village. We'll have to spend the night there.'

'I can't let you do that—not alone,' Roger protested in a whisper of sheer horror.

'It'll be much easier if I go alone Roger,' Paula stated the unkind truth briskly. 'I'll be perfectly all right. Yes, I'll get wet,' she anticipated his next protest irritably, 'but that can't be helped. Now, put the high-beam on and leave it on until I disappear from sight, then switch it off and just keep the parking lights on,' Paula instructed rapidly not letting him get a word in. 'I shouldn't be all that long.' She flung the door open and leapt out before Roger could stop her, and heard his final protest as a distorted wail against the pounding rain.

She was drenched to the skin in seconds and shocked to the bone by the ferocity of the wind which she hadn't taken into account when she left the car. It was shock that made Paula go on. The rain-dispersed light of the high-beam was blotted out within a few feet of the car, and while it couldn't yet have been anywhere near nightfall, she could barely see a step in front of her and tripped almost immediately she was out of range of the light.

Struggling to her feet, Paula kept on walking but knew she hadn't a hope of making it to the village, and that very soon she was going to have to do something, either sit down and stay down before the wind bowled her over again, or possibly try to retrace her steps to the car.

Roger would be relieved if she came back; he had been beside himself when she climbed out of the car and would be having a seizure by now. Poor Roger, Paula thought miserably, it certainly had not been his day, and she had not made it any easier for him with her unreasonable anger that he hadn't told her about Mark's suspicion. In that moment she had forgotten about his proposal entirely and hadn't given a thought to his feelings of hurt and rejection. Was it any wonder that Roger had thrown in the towel on the disastrous day and couldn't think of anything more constructive than waiting for the rain to stop.

It had not been her day either, and it was Hugo's fault, his fault that she was stumbling blindly through the rain, his fault that Roger sat distraught in that monster of a car.

The twisted logic brought a surge of anger that spurred Paula on, and the road seemed easier to see all of a sudden too. The rain must be easing, Paula thought, and in the same moment she could have sworn she heard her own name drifting through the wind. The sound, the voice, came again and this time seemed so clear and so close that Paula actually turned around—and saw everything all at once, only nothing registered, not the headlights, car, nor the figure almost on top of her. 'Roger,' she greeted in happy surprise, as if she'd just come across him unexpectedly at a cocktail party. 'You've managed it.' Paula laughed idiotically through the water streaming down her face.

Amazingly, Roger turned into Hugo and the next thing Paula knew she was scooped off her feet, rushed to the car and practically hurled into it. Too dazed for anything else, all her mind could take in was that Roger was not there. 'Where is he? What have you done with him?' she yelled in a burst of hysteria as Hugo threw himself into the driver's seat and slammed the door behind him. His face was murderous and any other time Paula might have been alarmed, only she was too terrified for Roger to worry about herself. When Hugo didn't answer she hit him wildly on the shoulder in a mindless panic. 'What have you done with him?'

Hugo swore savagely as he caught her hand and flung it back into her lap. 'For God's sake stop belting me and calm down.'

'Where is he?' Imagination running riot, she had a terrible vision of Roger lying helpless by the side of the road, tossed out by a furious Hugo. In the craze-induced picture, she even had his glasses broken.

'He's all right. I didn't throw him out,' Hugo shouted at her in an uncanny display of mind-reading. 'Though heaven knows I should have. The damn fool is with Neil in the other car.' He turned on the ignition with a grinding wrench and the car sprang forward.

Too angry to be relieved, Paula rose like a tigress in Roger's defence. 'He's not a fool and don't you dare call him one. It's all your fault. If you hadn't let him take the car . . .'

'You're damn right it's my fault, and I'm a bigger fool than the pair of you put together,' Hugo returned in a vicious mutter, manoeuvring the car around in a complicated U-turn. 'But if you hadn't been such an idiot and encouraged him, this would never have happened. I could have taken him for a drive and it would have been enough to get his fetish out of his system. Instead——' Hugo broke off, muttering.

'He was extra careful of your stupid car,' Paula screeched above the combined roar of the engine, swishing wipers, the rain, and whatever Hugo was muttering under his breath. 'It hasn't even got a scratch on it, as you'll find out when you go over it with your magnifying glass tomorrow.'

'You're unbelievable, do you know that?' Hugo hissed in mock amazement. 'Hasn't it penetrated your thick little skull that everyone was worried? How do you think I would have felt if anything had happened to you or your wretched fiancé? And if you couldn't care less about that, you might have considered my father. You're damn lucky you were spotted taking the turn for the Butt road or I wouldn't have known where to begin looking for you when the rain started. It would have served you idiots right if . . .' He cut off his tirade abruptly. 'Oh hell, I'm sorry,' he muttered tersely and fell silent.

It had not crossed Paula's mind to wonder how Hugo happened to turn up, nor, to her shame, had she given a thought to how worried Sir Iain might be—let alone Hugo. Chastened, she slumped miserably in the seat, water pouring down her back from her hair, streams of it trailing down behind her ears and down her neck, while the wet curls clung like red leeches to her forehead and cheeks. Paula stared bleakly down at her knees at the patches of mud, then at her grazed hands and remembered she had fallen. She sat up suddenly and shifted to the very edge of the seat so that she was almost overhanging the dashboard.

Hugo shot out an arm and pushed her roughly back into the seat. 'What now? Want to go through the windscreen?'

'I'm wet in case you haven't noticed, and dirty because I fell over. You wouldn't want me to mark your lovely suede, would you?' Paula replied, trying to sound sarcastic but succeeding only in sounding teary.

'I wouldn't—what?' Hugo quite yelped at her. He took his eyes off the road to stare at her.

Through the hair plastered over her forehead, Paula stared back belligerently. She was a sight and she knew it, but Hugo was looking at her as if she had gone mad to boot. He shook his head, bewildered, then his eyes flickered with what seemed to be faint alarm and he said, 'That's all right, Paula. I can get the suede cleaned.' He said it very kindly, soothingly, and with no trace of anger—like humouring someone a bit odd who might possibly turn dangerous. 'Don't worry about anything. Just sit back and I'll have you home in no time.'

Paula's bottom lip was quivering uncontrollably. She thought at first that everything was catching up with her and she was going to start howling in front of him, then the next moment, she was quivering—shaking, more like, all over. Her whole body was racked by the great waves of shivering. The car was warm yet the shivering just went on and on; her teeth were chattering and when Paula opened her mouth to speak, her teeth nicked her tongue in a spiteful little bite. She clenched her mouth tightly, fighting to get some control over the shaking.

When she was sure she could get words out without biting off her tongue, she said in a small uneven voice, 'We didn't mean to cause you so much trouble.'

Hugo's reply to that was to give a frustrated click of his tongue and throw her a quick glance. Paula hunched herself up and shivered violently for the rest of the way and neither of them said another word until the car sped up the drive to the house. Hugo screeched it to a stop outside the front door. 'Come on, we've got to get you inside before you collapse.'

Paula shook her head frantically. 'No ... n ... not the house ... please.' She felt wretched and looked worse and couldn't face the thought of parading herself in front of everyone in her miserable state.

Hugo's eyes sized up her agitation. 'The cottage then.' He restarted the car with a roar and eased it as far as he could along the drive around the side of the house to where the path to her cottage began.

'I can walk,' Paula told him hastily when Hugo helped her out of the car, thinking he was going to carry her again.

He let her stay on her feet—just; the arm around her waist was nearly lifting her off the ground as Hugo rushed her down the path through the driving rain that had him almost as wet as she was when they burst into the cottage.

Hugo flicked the switch by the door and flooded the cottage with reassuring light. In a moment he had turned on the electric heater.

'Th ... thank you. I ... I'll be fine now,' Paula chattered out the obligatory words of thanks.

Ignoring her, Hugo disappeared into the bathroom and Paula stood where he left her, inanely thinking that he must have been in a terrible hurry to get to the bathroom, when he came out almost immediately with a couple of towels in his hands. Then she wondered why he was going to bother drying himself when he'd get drenched again getting back to the house.

Hugo tossed the towels on to the table and swung around to her. 'Out of those clothes—quickly.'

'What are you . . .?' Paula began, puzzled. Her mind was not exactly functioning at full speed and Hugo's hands were on her, grabbing at the bottom of her sweater before Paula realised what he was about to do. 'No!' She hit out at him. 'Don't you dare.'

'You've got to get out of these wet things.' Hugo rasped at her.

'I . . . I'll do it. I'll do it.' Paula swatted at him ineffectually with hands that felt like they were encased in boxing gloves. 'I . . . I can do it.'

'When you're shivering so much you can't even land a decent swipe on me?' Hugo retorted with grim humour and the rest of her protest was lost in dank-smelling wool as the sweater came off over her head.

The spencer Paula wore underneath for warmth stuck wetly to her breasts in a parody of the wet tee-shirt sexiness favoured by girlie magazines. Hugo whipped it off without so much as a glance and snatching up a towel from the table, shoved it into her hands. 'Rub yourself down with this,' he ordered, his own hands already working at the fastening at her waist.

Outraged and humiliated, Paula stood helpless while the saturated, clinging jeans were dragged down over her hips and down her legs. She was shaking so much Hugo had to lift each foot up for her to get the shoes and jeans off while she made uncoordinated clutches at his wet pullover and hair to stop herself toppling over.

It was all done so quickly she was left in a daze but managed a final strangled wail of protest when he peeled off her skimpy pants. After that Paula fell silent, tears of misery running down her cheeks as Hugo attacked her with the towel, so roughly it hurt.

It only took seconds but her skin felt raw when he finished. Hugo plucked the towel out of her hand and wrapped it around her head. 'Don't just stand there, woman, dry your hair for heaven's sake.' He spun around and wrenched aside the curtain of the bedroom area. 'Where do you keep that damn bunny-rug?' he barked, then spotted the dressing-gown hanging from the hook on the wall beside the bed and snatched it up. He bundled her into it and took over on her hair.

'Ow . . . you're hurting me,' Paula whimpered, her ears on fire.

'Shut up.' Hugo gave her head one more vicious rub, flung the towel down and propelled her to the bed. Yanking back the bed-clothes, he pushed her down into it and whisked up the covers around her ears. 'Stay there,' he ordered, unnecessarily, since Paula was in no condition to go anywhere or do anything except shiver. The pillow-case felt like ice against the heat of her cheek and dampish where the tears were dripping on to it. She couldn't stop the crying any more than she could the shivering and after a moment, gave in to both of them and wallowed in sheer misery.

She missed hearing the click of the switch but knew the light had been turned off from the change of sensation behind her tightly-shut eyelids. Opening her eyes to the darkness, Paula waited for the sound of the door closing, vaguely surprised that Hugo was leaving without saying anything. And what had she expected? An apology for humiliating her? Hugo had stripped her like a six-year-old about to be flung into the bath after playing in the rain. She had never experienced anything more galling, and no apology could make her forgive him for the indignity.

In between the racking shivers, Paula pricked up her ears. She couldn't see a thing but became conscious of some sort of movement beside the bed. The bolt of alarm was pure instinct, then as Hugo climbed into the bed, she went so rigid with panic that for an instant the shivering stopped dead—and her mind with it.

Making inarticulate squeaks in her throat, Paula came out of her shock and tried to rear up from the pillow. Hugo wrapped his arms around her.

'Warmth, you idiot, you need warmth. Don't you realise that? Trust me for once. I'm not going to touch you.' Hugo railed at her in angry frustration.

If he had held her any tighter her ribs would have been at risk; Hugo seemed to be naked—or half naked, and their bodies could not have been more intimately entwined in the narrow bed than if they had been making love. And he was telling her he was not going to touch her? In the far reaches of her mind, Paula understood what he was trying to tell her but it took long moments for it to work through to her consciousness, before the struggle went out of her and she lay quite still in his arms.

Aware of the slackening of her body, Hugo released his hold slightly but still kept her pressed against himself as if afraid she was only decoying him before trying to spring out of the bed. Paula could feel the warmth of his body seeping through the wool of the dressing-gown and against her bare breasts where the dressing-gown gaped open.

'I was so worried.'

The murmur came from a long way away. The shivers were coming less and less frequently and each one less racking. Paula felt warm. Safe.

'Why don't you sleep now?' Hugo suggested softly. The idea of sleep was lovely but there was something drifting in and out of the fog in her mind; something she wanted to tell him. Paula remembered and was pleased.

'Roger and I are not engaged,' she said, suddenly pulling her face away from his chest, and felt Hugo's surprise in the way his hands made an abrupt tightening movement around her. 'We never were. He did ask me to marry him—today, not yesterday, like you thought. And I said no because I don't love him.' The voice was hers; matter-of-fact; emotionless. Paula could hear it very clearly saying these amazing things but it seemed to have nothing to do with her. Hugo must have been holding his breath because she couldn't feel the rise and fall of his chest against her. 'I never loved Mark either,' she went on, lifting the lid off the Pandora's box that was lodged in her head. 'I didn't realise it at first, but that must be why I kept putting off the wedding. And he kept trying to change me . . . into . . . I don't know. In the end I didn't even like him.'

Things kept coming out; things so repressed that Paula hadn't even been aware she had felt or thought that way until the words surfaced. About Mark and her crazy, mixed-up feelings, about the accident, her guilt; about not being able to draw for so long. And all the time Hugo listened in that utter silence while she exorcised her ghosts.

'It wasn't my fault—the accident. Mark knew—suspected, I wouldn't marry him. Roger told me today.' For the first time emotion came through in her voice, the same bewildered anger she had fleetingly unleashed at Roger. Paula started crying soundlessly. 'Why didn't Roger tell me earlier? I've wasted so much time being miserable, mixed-up. I haven't slept properly, the nightmare . . .'

'Won't come again.' Hugo's voice cut in fiercely through the darkness.

No, it wouldn't. Paula knew that too. She burrowed closer into his chest, overcome with weariness and relief. There was still something else; something that seemed important but it kept eluding her. It came at last. 'I love you, Hugo,' she murmured, satisfied, and thought she heard him say softly, 'I know,' but wasn't sure.

When Paula woke she was alone. Disconcerted, she turned her head towards the room, half-expecting to see Hugo. The curtain was still drawn to the side and the first thing she saw was Anna's scrawny back. Paula stared at it in perplexed dismay until the housekeeper must have sensed the eyes on her because she spun around from the table and looked to the bed. She's got her po-face on, Paula thought, before she wondered what the housekeeper was doing in the cottage at all.

'I've made your breakfast,' Anna said without preliminaries.

Making her breakfast was not something Anna had ever done for her before. 'Why?' Paula asked mechanically.

'Because Mr Cameron told me to, that's why.' No 'Mr Hugo'; it was 'Mr Cameron', and very tart at that.

So Hugo had ordered Anna to the cottage and the housekeeper was none too pleased about it. That explained Anna's presence and the bad temper. It explained something else too; Hugo couldn't disappear fast enough. The previous night was a half-remembered blur, but one thing stood out in embarrassing clarity; she had told Hugo she loved him and he hadn't even risked staying around to give her a chance to explain she hadn't meant it—that it had been shock or something. It must have been. In the cold light of morning the whole thing seemed preposterous; she did not love Hugo Cameron, Paula told herself angrily; she'd run a mile if she thought there was any danger of falling in love with him. Hugo was another man with a child, and she had been through all that before, thank you very much. Then why was she feeling so hurt, let down, by Hugo's absence—very pointed absence?

'That was very kind of him—and of you, but quite unnecessary,' Paula said with a weak smile that cost her a lot of effort.

Anna gave a huffy sniff. 'I'm sure I don't mind since Mr Cameron thought it so necessary,' she replied and looked as if she was sucking on a lemon.

An ache was starting behind Paula's forehead; she felt drained and jaded and not in the mood for one of Anna's standard huffs. She sat up, remembered her state of undress and hastily drew the fronts of the dressing-gown together. 'There's no need for you to stay, Anna. I'm perfectly all right.'

'So I see,' Anna observed sourly, 'but it would seem Mr Cameron thought otherwise, and that being the case he should have brought you into the house last night instead of . . .' She broke off, lips pinched up into a little furrowed circle of disapproval.

'Yes, Anna? Do go on. Instead of what?' Paula

inquired icily, her face flaring by angry contrast. Anna glowered back.

'Here on this island, Miss, we observe proprieties—old-fashioned as that might seem to some folk.'

Paula climbed out of bed very calmly, not quite sure whether she was actually going to hit the old lady when she reached her or bundle her out of the cottage by the scruff of her skinny neck. 'And what has your hyper-active imagination worked out happened here last night, Anna?' Paula asked with a dangerous pleasantness that made the housekeeper edge away from the table.

'That's not for me to say, and I wasn't saying anything happened,' Anna muttered defensively, doing a kind of sideways swirl towards the kitchen as Paula advanced on her. Then in an abrupt change of mind Anna pulled up short and stood her ground defiantly. 'It's not proper for a young lady to be put to bed by a gentleman, that's what I say.' She came out with it in a burst of belligerent self-righteousness.

And that was just the half of it. The other half would have stood the grey hair on its moralistic end, and for a moment Paula was sorely tempted to give the old lady the complete picture—and a likely heart attack; only the brief moment of malicious satisfaction would not have been worth the humiliation of Anna knowing what had really happened.

'How is Roger?' Paula changed the subject pointedly and felt a vague guilt that she had only just remembered to ask.

Anna came off her high-horse grudgingly. 'He's

all right,' she answered gruffly. 'Subdued, but I
don't think it was your caper in the car that's
responsible for that. He's leaving today, I gather,
but he'll probably come by to tell you that himself.'

'Poor Roger,' Paula murmured softly—to
herself, she thought, without allowing for the
sharpness of Anna's ears.

'Yes, he's that right enough,' Anna agreed,
shrewd old eyes fixed on Paula's face. Paula
stared back blandly.

'Young Jamie was at the door earlier wanting
to see you. I shooed him away but he's bound to
be back, and Sir Iain will be along later too, I
dare say, to check you out. Quite a busy morning
you'll be having with all your visitors, won't
you?' The tartness sprang back.

'For heaven's sake Anna, stop it!' Paula
snapped in irritation. 'I'm sorry you've been put
to so much bother. Thank you for making my
breakfast but I'm sure you're needed back at the
house, so don't let me detain you any longer,'
Paula sniped heatedly. 'And you needn't worry
that I'll be offending your island's morals and
good name for much longer because I intend to
leave today too.'

Anna's wrinkled features took on a sudden
pinkness. 'There's no need to carry on so. I'm
sure I didn't mean . . .'

'I know exactly what you meant.' Paula didn't
let her finish. 'And if it's any satisfaction to you,
it offended my senses of propriety too, to be put
to bed by a gentleman as you call him.'

'Well!' Anna sucked in her breath through her
teeth.

'Go away Anna. Please.' Paula appealed wearily, sick of the sight of the old lady and her innuendos.

'Now don't take on so, lass. I didn't mean to upset you,' Anna urged placatingly. 'I'm an old woman and you mustn't mind what I say. I'll stay and run your bath for you while you have some breakfast. Mr Hugo said ...' She hesitated. 'Come and eat,' she coaxed, placing a hand on Paula's arm.

Paula shook it off. 'Mr Hugo said—what?' she demanded sharply. What tactful little message had Hugo left, she wondered, bitterly.

'Nothing lass. Only that he'll be back soon. He had to go into town to make a telephone call because our wires came down in the storm last night and he wanted to get in touch with Miss ...' She caught back the name—not quickly enough. 'With somebody,' she finished rather lamely.

Paula smiled wincingly. 'Why so discreet, Anna? I presume the somebody is Miss Hunt, and Mr Cameron is welcome to get in touch with her where and when and as often as he chooses. That's his prerogative and I couldn't care less.'

That was not the way she was sounding. And not the way she was feeling either, which was hurt, resentful, and downright jealous.

The bath was ready when Paula finished picking at her toast. In the corner by the tub, her clothes of the previous evening were stacked up into an incongruously neat soggy little pile. Paula eyed them with distaste, mortified that Hugo had lavished such housewifely concern over them instead of kicking them into the nearest corner.

CHAPTER NINE

AFTER the bath her body felt better but the quick hot soak had not done anything much for the mess inside her head and the only thing half-way clear was that she had to get herself off the island and away from Hugo. She had made too much of a fool of herself last night, and practically every other time they'd been together if it came to that. No more.

Paula threw on her dressing-gown and after a rummage in the kitchen, found a plastic bag large enough to accommodate the offending damp clothes of the night before. Anna was gone and she flew about unhindered gathering her bits and pieces and throwing them unceremoniously into the case. She was on her knees, muttering to herself in irritation as she pushed the heaps of clothes this way and that to make room for the plastic bag, when for no particular reason, Paula suddenly glanced up to find Hugo watching her from the doorway and nearly jumped out of her skin. With all her concentration on what she was doing she hadn't heard the door open and had no idea how long he had been there.

Flusing guiltily, Paula scrambled to her feet clutching the lapels of the dressing-gown—again, and wishing she'd taken the precaution of dressing before she started the packing. 'I'm packing,' she said in a tone of voice used to reply to a question even though Hugo had not asked one.

Hugo's eyes hadn't left her face. 'So I see,' he said expressionlessly as he came into the room. There was nothing in his manner that was overtly threatening yet Paula instinctively made a dart past him so that they in fact reversed places—she at the kitchen end by the door, and Hugo near the suitcase by the bedroom area.

Dressed as she was she had nowhere to go and the room had never seemed so small. It was claustrophobic. Paula remained at her end aware that Hugo was watching her every move and taking care to avoid eye contact with him while she hurriedly tried out opening lines in her head. 'Look, about last night . . . I hope you didn't take me seriously.' Laugh. 'I'm not sure what I said last night, but . . .'

'What's all this about, Paula?' Hugo broke into her mental rehearsal with controlled testiness.

Paula flicked him a nervous glance. 'I'm leaving.'

Hugo crossed the room in a couple of strides. Paula was standing with her back against the kitchen counter. He placed both hands on the counter, hemming her in between them. 'That much I've gathered. I want to know why,' he said, very patiently. Paula stared into his face without answering. 'After last night,' Hugo began.

'You'll have to forgive me,' Paula interrupted with a scratchy laugh, 'but I'm afraid I don't remember anything about last night,' she said, looking him straight in the eye. 'Anna mentioned that I was in a bit of a state and that you were very kind to me. I'm very grateful. Thank you,' she added primly. Her eyes were starting to feel very stary. 'I know you're a busy man and it's most kind of you to look in on me. I really do appreciate it.' The words spilled out in a positively gracious stream but Paula didn't have much clue what she was saying. Hugo's expression unnerved her. 'I hope I wasn't too much trouble,' she prattled on.

Hugo was breathing hard, each intake of breath flaring his nostrils with rhythmic evenness. 'Keep this up and I shall slap you, Paula,' he threatened without raising his voice.

Judging from his eyes there was a strong probability he would do just that.

'What do you want?' Paula muttered sullenly.

'I want to talk about last night,' Hugo replied quietly.

'And I told you I don't remember anything.' Paula took a chance and persisted with her lie, moving her body slightly against his arm to gauge whether she could push it aside and get away from him. The arm felt like an iron rod.

'A very convenient attack of amnesia. I don't happen to believe you.' Hugo shook his head. 'You can't take them back, Paula, all the things you told me last night . . .'

'Shock,' she retorted. 'Haven't you ever heard of it? Perfect strangers spill out secrets to each other when they're sitting in a plane they think is going to crash. I believe it's quite a common phenomenon.'

'True,' Hugo agreed reasonably. 'Only we

weren't about to take a nose-dive in a plane. You might remember you were safe in my arms and that you trusted me, and wanted me to comfort you.'

The laugh that came out of her mouth was horrible. 'Under the circumstances I would have been just as comforted by the Hunchback of Notre Dame, so don't flatter yourself that it meant anything.'

The hurt was in his eyes one moment, gone the next. 'And told him you loved him?' Hugo asked with soft anger.

His body was too close. The counter dug painfully into the back of her waist as Paula pulled further away from him. 'Probably,' she returned, indifferently, wrenching her neck back as far as it would go as Hugo brought his face closer.

Hugo laughed angrily. 'A real little expert at paring egos down to size, aren't you?'

'Maybe that's because I've picked up a few tricks from the real expert. Isn't it enough for you that you reduced me to the level of a helpless kid, stripped me, put me to bed and then had the satisfaction of hearing me blurt things you had no right to hear? Why do you have to come and rub my nose in it? Don't you think I feel humiliated enough already?' Paula's voice shook. She felt alarmingly like howling.

Hugo drew back suddenly, taking his hands off the counter. His eyes were wide with surprise— genuine surprise. 'Good grief, is that what's bothering you? The fact that I had to undress you and put you to bed?' He seemed to find it difficult to believe. 'Come off it Paula, we've got more important things to discuss than that.'

'Like what? Jamie?' The child's name popped out to Paula's own surprise.

'Jamie?' Hugo looked at her blankly. 'What the hell has the child got to do with this?'

Everything, Paula wanted to scream at him. Everything. If she had blurted out the truth last night when she told Hugo she loved him—and she was half-afraid that she had—then where did that leave her? Tangled up with another man with another kid, never sure where she stood; never sure she was loved or needed for herself. Loved? That was a laugh. Hugo had never mentioned the word to her. 'Well, if it's not Jamie, we haven't anything to discuss,' Paula said dismissively.

'What about us, Paula? There's something between us whether you want to admit it or not, and we have to discuss where we go from here,' Hugo pointed out, almost gently.

Paula twisted out a smile. 'Oh that. I can tell you that, no trouble. From here I go back to London a.s.a.p. It's of no interest to me where you go, but I'm sure Miss Whatsit will be only too happy to organise an itinerary for you—both of you that is. You should have asked her for it when you telephoned her this morning.'

Hugo stared, taken aback, then grimaced. 'Drat that interfering old crone,' he muttered.

'Goodness, was it supposed to be a secret?' Paula jeered blithely. 'Don't worry, Anna was very discreet. She didn't tell me anything I didn't know—or guessed.'

Hugo made a peculiar sound like a strangled groan and suddenly grabbed her away from the counter. He held her arms pinned hard to her sides, hurting her in the grip. 'Now you listen to me. Yes, I did go into town early this morning to ring Louise Hunt—about business, and if that's what's made you seize up with fury, not to say jealousy, then I'm flattered, or would be if it wasn't for the fact that you're hell-bent on bolting back behind that no-speaks barrier of yours. And I'm not having that. We're going to have this out.'

'Spare me another of your psychological analyses. I'm sick of them,' Paula hissed at him.

'And I'm sick to death of you jumping to your twisted conclusions. I did not hop out of this bed and go racing off to tell Louise that I'd been in it, or whatever your feverish little mind has concluded I couldn't wait to tell her. That's the trouble with you Paula, you latch on to something and hang on like a dog with a bone. When you're wrong you simply close your mind off and won't admit it. That's how you could have a relationship with someone like Mark Naughton—some relationship when he couldn't bed you once in fourteen months . . . or didn't he get a chance to try?' Hugo sneered with a nasty softness.

She hadn't told him that. That part of her relationship with Mark was so humiliating, nothing could have dragged it out of her—not even delirium. Hugo was making wild stabs in the dark—and hitting raw nerves with horrible precision. If her hands had been free she would have hit him. They weren't free and Paula felt helpless with fury. Her eyelids prickled. 'I wondered how long it would take you to start throwing Mark in my face,' she choked out scornfully and turned away from him before the tears could spill out.

Hugo released her arms. 'And I'm going to throw a lot more in your face before I'm finished,' he muttered. 'About me, for instance. You decided I was a heartless monster, a womaniser, and God only knows what else, before you'd even met me. Damn it, Paula, when you burst into the hall that day with Jamie, I thought you were the most beautiful woman I'd seen and you looked at me as if I was something that had just slithered out from under a rock. But the attraction was there, Paula, and it didn't take you long to realise it, only then of course, you had to camouflage it, use Jamie.'

'What?' Paula spun back to him.

Hugo contemplated her shocked face with malicious satisfaction. 'You were going to use Jamie when you changed your mind and offered to look after him as I'd asked.'

She stared so hard her eyes felt on stalks. 'Are you implying I did that so I could be around you?'

'Yes, I am,' Hugo replied, infuriatingly calm.

'You're mad,' Paula spluttered, shaken, because the repressed suspicion about her own motives sprang forward in her mind and she remembered the peculiar disappointment she had felt when Hugo told her he didn't want her for the job after all. She remembered, too, how easy it had been for him to persuade her to stay when she had said she was leaving. She had already questioned herself about that, but not about offering to look after Jamie. What if what Hugo said was true, really true? What sort of hypocrite did that make her? Paula could not stand the scrutiny of the dark eyes boring into hers. She moved past Hugo abruptly and went to the table and sat down.

Hugo followed her to the table. 'It's me you want, Paula. When you told me last night that you loved me, you meant it. It had nothing to do with shock, deny it all you like.

'I do,' Paula shot back, not meeting his eyes.

'Of course you do,' Hugo agreed with a sneer in his voice. 'But you can lie until you're blue in the face and it won't change a thing because actions speak louder than words, and you gave me enough evidence before last night of how you really feel about me.'

Paula lifted her face to him angrily. 'I was drunk,' she burst out as the uncontrollable images and sensations rushed the red up her cheeks and right into her scalp.

'Not so drunk you didn't enjoy everything I did to you,' Hugo said coolly. 'And you weren't drunk the night I came back, when you wanted me to make love to you, nor the night we came back from the pub.' He looked down at her, taunting her with a smile, and the shiver of humiliated fury that shot through her made Paula want to kill him.

'Then you should have taken the opportunity while you had it,' she shouted.

Hugo laughed. 'And have you yell "rape" two

minutes later? You're so uptight about your own sexuality you'd have had to foist the blame on me, and I wasn't going to have you that way, certainly not your first time.'

Oh God, had she told him that too? Paula gaped at him, her face on fire. How much more had she burbled out last night?

'When we make love it's going to be because we both want to, Paula, not because your frustrations get the better of you and you can't help yourself.'

'Don't hold your breath,' she bit out with all the venom she could muster. 'You've missed your chance to get me to bed, and missed the chance to get a nanny for Jamie at the same time. It's too late now. I told you before I'm not interested in playing mummies and daddies with you. You'll just have to work harder on one of your other girlfriends now, won't you? I'm leaving.'

She thought he would hit her and realised it took a lot for him not to. Hugo was clenching and unclenching his fists as they stared at each other in the long angry silence. He studied her hostile face intently as if searching for something in it, then frowned and shook his head as if he couldn't find whatever it was he was looking for.

'You win Paula. I give up,' Hugo said with a sudden bitter weariness. 'I thought I understood you; it seems I don't.' He shrugged dispiritedly. 'God knows I've tried, but I haven't got a clue what's going on inside your head.' He bent over her, angry again. 'I'm me, Paula, not Mark Naughton in disguise. And yes, I do have responsibility for a child. I can't change that—

and wouldn't even if I could. Jamie's part of my life now, and if you can't accept that, well then, yes, I think you're right.'

Paula lifted her brows questioningly at him, not certain what Hugo was talking about, what she was supposed to be right about.

'You're right, Paula,' he repeated for her. 'I think you should leave. Only don't think I'll be coming looking for you—I won't. The next move is up to you. If you ever sort yourself out, let me know.'

She watched him walk to the door and had the awful sense of watching him walk out of her life, and would have given anything to stop him but couldn't. Pride, the old distrust, the old insecurity all mingled together; the barrier was well and truly up. When Hugo turned from the door to look at her, Paula presented a hard frozen mask, which was how she felt inside. Cold and hard, but brittle too, as if she was going to crack into a million tiny pieces.

'I'll tell Neil he'll have another passenger for the airport, shall I?' Hugo said with toneless politeness. His face, Paula guessed, looked like her own.

'Thank you, yes,' she enunciated frigidly, still not believing that he was doing this to her, expecting, hoping, that before the door closed he would stride back across the room and take her in his arms and everything would be all right— somehow; that he would sweep all her doubts away from her, somehow.

Paula sat at the table for a long time after Hugo had gone, not thinking about anything, her mind

quite soothingly blank until the sight of the open
suitcase on the floor penetrated her consciousness
at last. And then she whirled about at a great
pace, getting dressed, tidying up and finishing
the packing moments before Neil turned up to
take her suitcase and folders to the house.

She left with Roger on the midday flight. Sir
Iain was the only one to see them off from the
house and it was a subdued, embarrassing, no-
questions-asked leave-taking. Paula murmured
her thanks and something about keeping in touch
and couldn't leave quickly enough. Only later did
she remember that there had been no sign of
Hugo's car, which meant Hugo had gone off in it,
and presumably taken Jamie with him since there
had been no sign of the child either. That had
been a relief. She did not know how she would
have coped with saying goodbye to Jamie or
explaining her sudden departure because she
hadn't worked out what there was to explain, let
alone how, to the child who in some illogical way
she felt stood between herself and Hugo.

She would come up with something and
explain it in a letter, Paula decided, and three
weeks later still hadn't written. All she had
managed to do was send the briefest of thank-you
notes to Sir Iain and it took her a couple of days
after she'd sent it to realise the ulterior motive
behind that little bit of courtesy. She was staying
with her parents at the farm and wanted Sir Iain
to know that—or rather, wanted Hugo to know,
just in case. Just in case what?

Rationally, she did not expect to hear from
Hugo; told herself she did not want to hear from

him; that she had to put Hugo and the island behind her and get on with her life, her work.

Work was a godsend and Paula worked like someone possessed, driving herself almost to the point of exhaustion every day so that when she fell into bed there was no gap to fill with thoughts before she lapsed into heavy dreamless sleep, and in the morning was at the drawing-board again with a frenzied energy. It was as if nothing else in the world mattered except the illustrations.

'You're working too hard, Paula.' Her mother had slipped into Paula's studio unnoticed and Paula started jerkily at the sound of her voice.

Mrs Halstead frowned at the nervous move-ment. 'Sorry, I didn't mean to startle you.'

'You didn't,' Paula lied, embarrassed and angry for the uncontrollable reaction. Her nerves were like guitar strings about to snap and lately every unexpected sound made her jump. 'I was just concentrating.'

'Can't you take it a little easier, darling? Surely Roger can wait another week or two.' Karen Halstead's smile couldn't cover up the anxiety in her eyes.

Paula's work had nothing to do with Roger any more. Roger had disappeared from her mind so completely that she had to make a conscious effort to connect him with the illustrations at all. 'I want to get the last few finished, a couple more days should do it.' Paula gave her mother what she hoped passed for a reassuring smile.

'And then?' The older woman did not smile back. 'What then, Paula?'

Paula was afraid to think about that. More work? There would always be more work. She would ask Roger for something else when she took in the finished artwork to him. 'I think Roger has something else for me—now that I've got my touch back, so to speak,' Paula said lightly but faint bitterness showed through in her voice willy-nilly. She could draw again; her stay on the island had achieved that much at least

Mrs Halstead arranged her long, jean-clad legs under her, settling into the studio's one armchair with the air of someone about to stay a while. Paula tried not to show her annoyance. Her mother had been great—asked no questions when she must have been dying to do so. It was too good to last and the questions had to come sooner of later.

'You know, Paula.' Karen Halstead studied her daughter carefully. 'When you came home you looked marvellous, and I thought, well, I thought everything was all right again. You looked so much like your old self.'

This was familiar territory. Roger had said something to the same effect too. The only trouble was Paula didn't know any more what that 'old self' had been like—or if she wanted to be that self again.

Her mother was twirling a strand of the gorgeous red hair absent-mindedly, eyes still on Paula's face.

'But something is still wrong, something else, isn't it? It's not Mark or Stephen any more, I can sense that.' A whimsical little smile flitted over her face. 'I'm not that scatty you know, dear, that I can't see how things are.'

'I never assumed you were,' Paula replied crossly. She had long ago seen through her mother's endearingly vague façade. It was just that—façade; behind it was a very astute lady whose beautiful green eyes didn't miss much.

'Don't be cross with me, Paula. I don't want to pry; I'm just concerned.'

'I know,' Paula mumbled miserably, and just for a moment wished she could pour out her misery into a sympathetic ear. Paula got up from the drawing board and, moving to her mother's side, kissed the porcelain-white skin of the cheek under the vibrant hair. 'Please don't worry about me.'

'If you ever do want to tell me . . .' Her mother's voice trailed away. The elongated green eyes stayed troubled.

'I will,' Paula murmured hastily, and knew she wouldn't, and guessed by the sigh that her mother knew that too.

And what was there to tell? That she was miserable because she had run away from a man and regretted it, and now, contrarily, wanted him to come searching her out even though he had told her he wouldn't, even though she wasn't really sure how she felt about him. Not deep down. There were still so many doubts. Yes, she found him immensely attractive; yes, she did want to go to bed with him. But all that was purely a physical reaction. Her mind, the rational part of it, kept trotting out the warnings to leave well alone.

Her mother uncurled herself from the armchair and drifted aimlessly around the studio, pausing to cast a professional eye over Paula's work as she passed. Nothing Karen Halstead did was ever really without purpose. Paula watched her expectantly. At the door her mother turned, as if something had only just occurred to her.

'When you've handed the work in to Roger, will you come to Italy with me?' she asked, casually. 'There's a new exhibition of Firelli sculptures on in Rome and your father is too busy to come,' she rushed on breathlessly. 'I'd love the company, we could do some shopping.'

Italy. Paula might have guessed; her mother's panacea for anything and everything. And yet, facile as it was, it could solve a lot of problems. Paula was dreading the blank that would come after the commission was finished. There was always a let-down phase to get through after any commission and it would be worse this time. Italy. Paula turned the idea over in her mind. Exhibitions, trailing around the galleries, churches; shopping till their feet were ready to drop off; long, lazy evenings in cafés and artists' studios. Paula gave her mother a sudden smile. 'Yes, I'd like that,' she said brightly on a wave of relief that a ready-made solution for keeping Hugo Cameron out of her mind had presented itself so easily.

Only it didn't quite work out that way. Somehow the distance made it worse because a new note crept into Paula's thoughts of Hugo and she found herself worrying incessantly—about how Hugo was coping with Jamie, whether he'd found someone yet to look after the child; whether he'd managed to sort out all the business problems, and small, silly things like whether Hugo was getting enough rest, eating properly.

It was those unexpected small concerns that finally brought it home: sexual attraction doesn't make anyone worry about a man, not the way she was doing. She cared about Hugo Cameron—desperately—and was very frightened that she'd lost him through her own stupidity and immaturity.

It was her hopeless insecurity about herself that had made her act as if she hated him and resort to denying her true feelings—to herself as much as Hugo. She hadn't been able to believe Hugo could return those feelings, that he could be interested in her for herself. Mark had seen her primarily in terms of a stepmother, not a wife, but Hugo was not Mark. He had told her that—or tried to, at their last angry meeting. Yes, he was another man with a child, but half a dozen children hanging around his neck couldn't make the slightest difference to how she felt about him.

They had come to Italy for six weeks; at the end of the second week Paula flew back to England. She went straight to her own flat in London, and leaving the suitcase where the cab driver had left it in the hall, sprang to the telephone to ring her father at the farm. Lingering at the back of her mind was the unbearable hope that there would be some word from Hugo. There wasn't and she felt shattered. The hasty decision to cut short the holiday no longer seemed the good idea it had been at the time. The doubts came thick and fast. What if she had left it too late and Hugo didn't care any more? What if she had never been anything more than a passing attraction anyway, just someone to bed for a night or two?'

But Hugo hadn't bedded her, Paula reminded herself with a small surge of hope. He could have, but hadn't taken advantage of her inexperience and frustrations. Surely that meant something. What? That he had cared, or not cared enough? Paula pushed the last thought out of her mind. There was only one way to find out, to settle things between them once and for all and it terrified her. 'The next move is up to you,' Hugo had told her. Well, she was about to make that move.

It was early evening with the shadows only beginning to lengthen. The air was still full of warmth but without the engulfing heaviness of the Italian summer evenings she had just left behind. After a hurried bath Paula dressed carefully. She had bought new clothes in Rome— her mother had seen to that, but there was a difference this time: they were all Paula's choice—her own style, not her mother's flamboyant purchases in which Paula felt overwhelmed, nor Mark's dreary notions of good taste which left her feeling reduced to a drab shadow. The clothes seemed to say, I'm Paula Halstead—at last; take me or leave me.

Paula put on an olive green textured linen skirt and a loose-fitting cream silk shirt. Her hair had been trimmed—ecstatically, by a frenziedly artistic young man in one of Rome's top salons, and her skin glowed with soft golden colour. Paula knew she looked great but felt terrible, and the only way she could even think of acting on her decision was to keep telling herself that Hugo was on the island or somewhere in New York and it was only an old housekeeper she was going to see.

Even then she took the coward's way out. She had bought a present for Jamie—a box of construction blocks, a sort of Italian version of Lego, and intended to use that as the excuse for the call. She would leave the present with the housekeeper and Hugo would know she had made the move. Of sorts. It was a roundabout way of doing it but just the fact that she had turned up on his doorstep should be enough to tell him she was sorry. It had to be, because Paula simply didn't have the courage to tell him any other way.

She knew the address; Sir Iain had given it to her when he had gone to London with Hugo, but when the cab dropped her off, Paula's nerve momentarily failed her and instead of going to the door, she went across the road to the square's garden. There was a bench almost directly opposite Hugo's house and she sat on that, playing with the box on her lap and telling herself she was an idiot for being so nervous. The housekeeper was hardly going to spring questions on her or put her through the third-degree before accepting a present for the child; that sort of thing was Anna's speciality, and mercifully that curiosity-riddled little crone was hundreds of miles away on a remote island.

Rehearsing her lines, Paula recrossed the road at last. She was going to be super-casual—breezy, was the word. '. . . just passing by and . . .'

She had barely touched the brass knocker when the door was flung open by Hugo.

CHAPTER TEN

'I was just passing by.' The rehearsed lie came automatically. Unaware she'd even spoken, Paula's eyes were on Hugo's face, taking in the difference made by the six weeks or so that she hadn't seen him. Hugo looked older and almost drawn. His hair needed a trim and under the T-shirt tucked carelessly into his jeans, he seemed to be thinner. She had been right: Hugo hadn't been getting enough rest or eating properly. Her mind registered every detail of him like an instamatic camera, then Paula realised she was staring and that Hugo was staring back at her in pretty much the same way, with the same sort of fixed intensity. And yet there was something else about his expresion too—or possibly something missing from it that Paula couldn't quite put her finger on.

'I didn't think you'd . . . I wasn't expecting you to be home,' she mumbled in a fluster and jerkily thrust the colourfully-wrapped box at him. 'For Jamie. I was just passing by and . . .'

'So you said.' Hugo took the parcel with one hand, her elbow with the other. 'Come in, won't you?' The tone of the voice did away with any connotation of the words being a polite invitation, and his grip was too firm to be the casual gesture of the polite host about to shepherd his guest inside.

'No, oh no,' Paula returned hastily. 'I was just passing.' She snapped off the phrase that was starting to sound like a track with the needle stuck in it and allowed herself to be drawn into the hall then stayed silent as Hugo led the way up the stairs and into a large sitting-room on the next floor.

The first thing that caught and held her eyes when Paula came into the room was the enormous window that took up most of one wall. Its heavy drapes to the sides, it gave anyone standing near it a bird's-eye view of the gardens across the road—and the bench where she had sat gathering up her courage. The perplexing feeling about Hugo's reaction at the sight of her on his doorstep clarified itself in an instant. Hugo had shown no surprise at seeing her when he should have been surprised. Paula tossed him a quick glance. Hugo's face gave nothing away; his eyes carefully avoided the window and she knew immediately that he had been watching her from that very window for at least some of the time. The realisation didn't do much for what was left of her self-possession.

'Won't you sit down,' Hugo suggested, courteously.

Paula looked about uncertainly, picked on a straight-backed chair which was furthest away from the window and sat down on the edge of it.

'Drink?' Hugo offered and she nodded a jerky assent and dropped her eyes to her lap.

This was wrong, all wrong, Paula thought despairingly. She had made the move and whatever fib she had produced to account for it,

Hugo must know what that move meant. And he was acting like a stranger—polite to his back teeth. Their last emotion-charged encounter with its intimate anger seemed like a figment of her imagination, as unreal as her expectation that the next time they met Hugo would simply gather her into his arms and ... She must have been crazy.

Paula looked up to take the proffered drink and watched bleakly as Hugo returned to the drinks cabinet. What was she supposed to say or do, now?

With his own drink in hand, Hugo turned around to face her. Paula hurriedly averted her eyes and as she did so her glance flicked off Jamie's present on the coffee-table where Hugo had put it. 'How is Jamie?' she asked, pouncing on the subject of the child with a desperate brightness.

'Fine.'

'Where is he?'

'In bed.'

'Here?' Paula was surprised enough to moment-arily meet Hugo's eyes.

'Yes. I brought him down with me a couple of weeks ago when I got back from the States. He's settled in quite well and I shouldn't need to return to America for a good while yet, if at all,' Hugo volunteered casually.

'That's nice,' Paula murmured mechanically. Part of her mind noted the fact that Hugo must have ironed out his business problems and she was quite genuinely glad for him. Under different circumstances she would have liked to tell him so;

under present circumstances she didn't know how.

In the drawn-out silence Paula studied the room; a masculine room but with warmth. The furnishings were a mixture of antique and modern; a comfortable blend and she liked it.

'Did you finish the illustrations?' Hugo asked conversationally, and to Paula the question sounded like a conversation gap-filler; just something to fill the silence with no real interest behind it. More fool her for expecting some.

Cutting off her inspection of the room, Paula glanced at him briefly. 'Yes, I did,' she replied shortly and looked down at her lap. She held her drink tightly with both hands and felt sick inside. Her worst fears were true. If Hugo had ever been interested in her he certainly wasn't any more. She had one consolation though, albeit a very small one, and that was that she hadn't flung herself into his arms on the doorstep and blurted out everything, that she loved him; that she was sorry she had hurt him. That would have been the final humiliation; just sitting here and being treated to a dose of Hugo's detached politeness was bad enough. Paula put down the barely-tasted drink on the small wine-table by the chair and sprang to her feet.

'You're looking very well,' Hugo said, ignoring her sudden move. 'Italy must have suited you.'

Hardly listening, Paula muttered a distracted, 'Thank you. Yes,' and headed for the door. 'I must go. I was just passing by.' It came out again before she could catch it and she could have kicked herself for doing herself out of a cool dignified exit. 'Thank you for the drink,' she added in a mumble, desperate to get out of the room.

She had reached the door before Hugo's words penetrated; one word, rather: Italy. Paula stopped. Italy. How did Hugo know she had been to Italy? She hadn't written to Sir Iain from Rome—not even sent a postcard. Roger knew she had gone there, and her family of course, but the only way Hugo could have found out was to have got in touch with one of them during the last two weeks. And that meant . . . Paula's thinking process was tortuous and slow and she almost had to spell out each word to herself. It meant Hugo had tried to reach her; that he had come after her without waiting for her to make the next move. Paula turned around slowly.

'You said you wouldn't be coming to look for me,' she accused. 'You said . . .'

'In which case I make almost as good a liar as you do, don't I?' Hugo's voice was gently mocking but there was an uncertain note in it just beneath the surface. The smile was uncertain too, as if Hugo wasn't at all sure what her reaction was going to be.

Paula wasn't sure either. Everything became a momentary jumble in her head. She was confused, piercingly happy, and unaccountably angry in lightning turn, and then she was across the room and in Hugo's arms without knowing how she got there.

Their mouths came together in a kiss that was an explosion of emotional violence and seemed to have nothing to do with love. There was anger in both of them and it surged out, demanding physical release. Hugo's mouth probed deeply and bruisingly, his hands hurt her back, and Paula responded with the same mindless intensity. Her mouth returned Hugo's fierceness; her fingers gripped and dug into his shoulders as if she wanted desperately to hurt him back, but underneath it all she recognised the love, hers, Hugo's; the tenderness would have to come later.

Passion exhausted at last, their hands stilled around each other while their lips stayed locked and motionless until Paula pulled her mouth away with abruptness.

'Why did you do that to me? Why did you make me sit through all that terrible politeness, deliberately let me think you didn't care any more?' she cried out reproachfully.

Hugo pressed his eyes shut and grimaced. He opened them and stared at her in confusion. 'I don't know. I didn't mean . . . I'm sorry,' he mumbled, reddening.

Paula gazed at him steadily and realised that deep down she understood, perhaps better than he did, what had made him act that way. Hugo was as vulnerable to hurt and uncertainty as anybody else and he had simply been protecting himself—and his bruised pride with that façade of stony politeness; behind it he had been as scared as she was.

'It's all right,' she said softly. 'I understand.'

'Then tell me you love me,' Hugo pleaded raggedly.

'I love you,' Paula obeyed in a husky little whisper and felt a tremor run through Hugo's body as the deep sigh of relief drained itself out of him and he dropped his head to bury his face in her shoulder. Very gently, Paula curved a hand around the back of his head and pressed him to her in the long sweet moment of silence.

Hugo lifted his head. 'I thought you'd never come,' he said wearily. 'I was going mad with the waiting and had to ring Harris last week to find out where you were because I couldn't stand it any longer, not knowing.' Hugo smiled shakily. 'And all the time you were just calling my bluff.'

Paula frowned into his face. 'Bluff?' she repeated incredulously.

Hugo gave a raspy laugh. 'You can't have believed I'd let you walk out of my life just like that? I'd have gone looking for you to the ends of the earth. I love you Paula—loved you from the moment I set eyes on you, don't you understand that?'

'But you sent me away—let me leave the island,' Paula amended, but it was all one and the same in her mind. Frustration flickered sharply. 'Why did you do that?' she demanded plaintively. 'We could have sorted this out six weeks ago without—everything.' Without the doubts and the torment, she meant. They could have been together weeks ago instead of being miserably apart.

'Could we? Have sorted it out? I don't think so, Paula.' Sensing her agitation, Hugo was serious. 'I realised that morning In had to give you space, time, to work things through for yourself—to see things clearly.'

'But if you had only told me you loved me

then,' Paula persisted heatedly. 'Really told me. You never did that. If you had . . .'

Hugo intervened with sudden sharpness. 'And would you have believed me? Wouldn't you have concluded it was some sort of ploy on my part to snare a nanny for Jamie, or that I was angling for a stepmother for the child?'

Paula couldn't answer immediately. She forced her mind back six weeks and made herself look at the irrational woman she had been. 'I don't know,' she mumbled at last. 'I honestly don't know what I would have thought, then.'

'But I do,' Hugo said firmly. 'You were so mixed-up, my darling, you drove me to despair. I thought I'd never get through to you. My main mistake was asking you to look after Jamie in the first place.' Hugo laughed, a little bitterly. 'At the time it seemed like a heaven-sent opportunity of ensuring that I kept you near me, but I didn't know then about your past involvement with Naughton and his child. Believe me, I would never have asked you if I'd known about them,' Hugo assured her earnestly. 'And then when you suddenly changed your mind I couldn't risk accepting your offer. I couldn't be sure of your reasons—whether it was me or simply Jamie you were interested in, although that became pretty clear soon enough—when you turned against both of us.' Hugo smiled, but what he was saying was not the least bit amusing. Paula winced.

'About Jamie, I didn't mean to,' she started, abashed.

'Jamie is part of my life, Paula.'

He had told her that before.

'I know. And I'm glad,' Paula replied softly. 'I love Jamie too.' A smile teased her lips. 'One child or six, it couldn't change the way I feel about you.'

Hugo grinned suddenly. 'Six? I hadn't planned on quite that many, but if you . . .'

She reached around his neck with her hands and brought his mouth down to hers. There was no shattering violence left in either of them. The kiss was lingering and unbearably tender. Paula wanted it to go on forever.

Hugo drew away from her. 'Marry me.'

'Yes,' Paula said simply, then added with a tiny laugh, 'I thought you'd never ask.'

The comment was meant to be light-hearted but Hugo didn't take it that way. 'I wanted to ask you that morning—our last morning together, after you'd finally told me about yourself . . . about your feelings for me,' he explained anxiously. 'Only I didn't get the chance because all your distrust of me was back—with a vengeance. What in heaven's name did that man do to you to make you so . . . so . . .' The word Hugo was searching for eluded him.

'Twisted?' Paula prompted matter-of-factly. Like it or not, that was the right word. She had been 'twisted'; twisted up in knots with distrust and guilt; her perception of herself and everybody around her had been twisted too. 'It wasn't Mark's fault—not entirely,' she admitted honestly. 'I was just confused about things, myself mainly; not knowing who I was or what I wanted.' Paula shrugged and said determinedly, 'I don't want to talk about Mark.'

Mark's memory was no longer threatening but Mark was the past and she didn't want to look back any more. She had spent a fruitless year doing just that but now she was ready for the present—and the future with Hugo.

'Good.' Hugo's happy laugh made him sound and look years younger. 'Neither do I.' He gathered her to himself closely, running his hands caressingly down the curve of her back. 'And we're never going to talk about that misunderstanding of mine about Harris either. Agree?'

'Agree,' Paula murmured into his chest, then yanked herself away from him with a jerk. 'I want to know about Louise Hunt,' she said, because at this moment it seemed very important to know. Louise, she realised, was still a block in her mind, big and black—or was it green for jealousy?

The unexpected mention of Louise's name brought momentary surprise to Hugo's face, then he grinned hugely with satisfaction. 'I love it when you're jealous; your eyes go a deep, deep green—very fetching,' he teased, and when Paula refused to return a smile Hugo's grin vanished. 'Listen Paula, I'm thirty-six years old and I can't—won't pretend that I've led a monastic life to date. I haven't,' Hugo said frankly, and wasn't telling her anything that Paula hadn't been able to work out for herself. Only Hugo's other women were shadows in his past and didn't count. Louise Hunt was uncomfortably real and for some inexplicable reason did count, surprisingly a lot.

'But,' Hugo continued with emphasis, 'Louise

Hunt has never been part of my private life. She's been my personal assistant for seven years and in all that time I have never made love to her,' Hugo told her, patiently, as if he was carefully explaining something to someone who might have difficulty understanding. 'I have never made love to Louise because I've never wanted to. In fact,' he added on an afterthought, 'I doubt if any man has bedded her for years. Louise is strictly a career lady and a very fine one at that. I couldn't have done without her these last few months since James's death and I've already nominated her for James's seat on the Board. Later, she'll be taking over the directorship of the American side of the business, and a jolly good job she'll make of it too. Does that set your little mind at rest?' The teasing note edged back.

'But Louise hated me,' Paula burst out, puzzled and not fully reassured; Hugo might not have been interested in Louise, but what about the reverse?

'Don't be so melodramatic,' Hugo laughed outright. 'Louise merely disliked you. Nothing personal; she disliked Jamie—and my father too, I dare say, because they take up my time; time which in Louise's book should be devoted exclusively to business. Louise is nothing if not single-minded. And she's very perceptive too. She knew the moment she saw you that you'd be taking up a lot of my time. And she was right— she usually is,' Hugo added, frankly impressed.

'Yes, but I still don't understand why.' Paula couldn't let go of the bone.

'Hush, that's enough.' Hugo placed a finger

over her lips and cut her off, and whatever Paula was about to say vanished from her mind. So did Louise. There was only Hugo and herself and Paula knew what was coming next; Hugo's eyes were telling her as they combed her face. She was aware her breathing had changed rhythm and her excitement was mounting under the promise and desire in Hugo's gaze.

'It's been a long wait, Paula,' Hugo said huskily.

Shy and all at once a little frightened, Paula moistened her dry lips with the tip of her tongue. She had never made love before and needed to tell him that, needed to explain things.

'Trust me, Paula.' It was a plea, question, command all rolled into one.

Hugo understood. The last barrier in her mind melted away without a trace. 'Yes,' Paula answered in a firm clear voice and closed her eyes with a contented sigh as she lifted her face for his kiss.

Harlequin American Romance
Harlequin celebrates the American woman...

...by offering you romance stories written about American women, by American women for American women. This series offers you contemporary romances uniquely North American in flavor and appeal.

◆

Harlequin Temptation
Passionate stories for today's woman

An exciting series of sensual, mature stories of love...dilemmas, choices, resolutions... all contemporary issues dealt with in a true-to-life fashion by some of your favorite authors.

◆

Harlequin Intrigue
Because romance can be quite an adventure

Harlequin Intrigue, an innovative series that blends the romance you expect... with the unexpected. Each story has an added element of intrigue that provides a new twist to the Harlequin tradition of romance excellence.

Harlequin Books

PROD-A-2